BLAZING BORDER

E. E. HALLERAN

SAGEBRUSH
Large Print Westerns

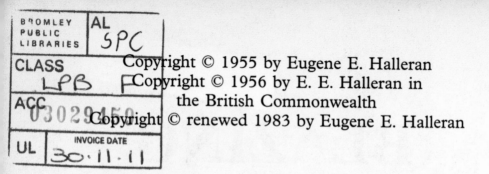
First published in Great Britain by Hammond
First published in the United States by Macrae Smith

Published in Large Print 2011 by ISIS Publishing Ltd.,
7 Centremead, Osney Mead, Oxford OX2 0ES
by arrangement with
Golden West Literary Agency

British Library Cataloguing in Publication Data
Halleran, E. E. (Eugene E.), 1905–
   Blazing border.
   1. Western stories.
   2. Large type books.
   I. Title
   813.5'4–dc22

ISBN 978–0–7531–8761–6 (pb)

Printed and bound in Great Britain by
T. J. International Ltd., Padstow, Cornwall

BLAZING BORDER

CHAPTER
ONE

The late afternoon sun glared down viciously, as if it took a personal interest in mocking the sea of dead browns it had created. The hot, thirsty land tried to glare back, but the result was only a lot of wriggling heat devils which made the hot afternoon seem hotter. It was one of those times when no one moved if he could avoid it, particularly if he had Spanish blood in his veins.

That was one of the reasons why the ragged man on the sleepy mule hesitated to approach the first cluster of huts which marked the southern fringe of San Antonio's Mexican quarter. After going to so much trouble to make himself look like a lazy peon, it was a bit out of character to be riding along a trail at a time when any self-respecting *mozo* would be taking his siesta.

"Not too much risk, I reckon," the man muttered to himself half aloud, his voice almost a croak as the whisper came from a dusty throat. "Nobody wants me — and the army's supposed to be in full force here. It oughta be safe enough." The words and the intonation were no more Mexican than were the notably light-gray eyes. There was a trace of Texas in the easy drawl, but at

1

the same time there was something else, an accent which was not too easy to identify.

Even as he spoke he made himself slump a little more in the saddle, his immense straw sombrero inclining another degree or two until it almost touched the long twitching ears of the mule. A man who worked the border had to recognize his own weak points and allow for them. To Fred Starke that meant voice and eyes. Long ago he had learned that people considered his enunciation a little odd. More frequently they had commented on the gray eyes, which seemed so unusual in the heavily tanned face with its dark brows. Today he had no business using his voice at all, even to mutter to himself. It was as foolish as letting people see his eyes.

He let the plodding mule amble slowly past the first group of shacks until presently the ground sloped upward and he could see a fringe of yellowish green which he knew would mark the confluence of the San Antonio and the San Pedro. Even in a dry season like this one, the river would retain enough moisture to keep vegetation alive along its banks. Somewhere along its course should be the camp to which he had been ordered to report.

Thought of that order still gave him a funny feeling. After three years without hearing from superiors he felt somewhat at a loss to be under orders once more. He was not too sure that he liked it.

From the top of the rise he could see the way the town had spread out during that three-year period. Off to the north he could make out the precise alignments of the army camp, company streets reaching completely out of sight beyond distant ridges. Down closer to the river were the permanent buildings which would be homes of both American and Mexican residents. The town had grown, even during war time.

He looked up only long enough to fix the scene in his mind, letting the mule drift lazily down the slope toward the next cluster of adobes. Two facts had been swiftly apparent to him. One was that the Mexican quarter had grown tremendously since his last visit. Refugees from the Maximilian government of Mexico had swarmed across the border, taking full advantage of the lack of immigration rules during the war between the states.

The second point of interest had been the army camp. Rumor on that score had evidently been true enough. The Federal government was supposed to be sending a large force to the Mexican border, a force large enough to drive the French and their puppet emperor out of Mexico. If this detachment in San Antonio was a sample of what was going on in other parts of Texas, the government must be serious about the project.

A dry chuckle that was not particularly mirthful came with the thought. Better not start jumping to conclusions, he told himself. Maybe the government needed this much of a force just to make certain that the Rebellion wouldn't break out again. After all, a Texas army had defeated a Federal force at Palmetto Ranche a full month after Lee's surrender in Virginia. Some of these Texans hadn't surrendered yet. Those lines of tents beyond the river might mean simply that the Federals still expected trouble in this region.

Before he could consider the point further his attention was distracted by something closer at hand. From the direction of the nearest bend of the river a rider appeared on a prancing white horse that looked very much like a thoroughbred. In a land of mustangs the horse itself was outstanding enough, but the rider added substantially to the interest. She was obviously young, apparently having a fine time, and doing an excellent job of controlling the horse.

"Crazy woman," Starke grumbled under his breath. "Got no business over here. Anyway, it's too hot."

The gap between them closed quickly as the young woman sent her mount along at a brisk pace. Starke had just decided that she was reasonably pretty when suddenly there came an interruption. Two bearded men on cow ponies swung into the trail from the cover of a pecan grove, ranging themselves across the open patch to block the girl's passage. If they saw the droopy-looking Mexican on the sleepy mule, they didn't seem to think him worthy of their attention.

"Drunk!" the mule rider growled between clenched teeth. "I hope they're not fixin' to make any trouble."

He knew as he spoke that the thought was vain. The bearded pair plainly intended to intercept the girl. For a moment she seemed to hesitate, as if she read their intention, then she put spurs to the white horse and tried to burst through their barricade. It was a bold effort, but the men were not to be denied. They acted clumsily but with decision, one grabbing the white

4

bronc's bridle while the other lurched in to put his arm around the girl and lift her bodily from the saddle.

Starke had pulled up sharply at the first move, irritation making him almost as angry at the girl as at the ruffians who had attacked her. There was nothing he wanted more than to avoid attracting attention to himself, but he could not hold back and permit these men to maltreat the girl. He glanced around, hoping that someone else might come to her rescue, even starting the mule toward the pecan clump in the hope that he would be able to ease himself out of the picture. But no other American had been foolish enough to leave shelter and cross the river this afternoon. No Mexican on this side of the stream seemed to be awake.

Actually there was no hut within four or five hundred feet, and when the girl screamed sharply, the sound brought no result. By that time her efforts had brought her close enough to Starke so that she made her appeal directly to him, trying to shout something past the grimy hand that covered her mouth.

In the effort to silence her the bearded man lost a stirrup and the pair of them went sprawling to the dusty trail, the other ruffian going into a spasm of laughter at the sight. He was just drunk enough to think that the whole thing was a huge joke, although his comment hinted that there was a malicious side to the humor:

"Snub her down hard, Eli! Don't let no Yankee filly git the best of ye. We'll learn them bluebellies not to come down here actin' so damn big. Roll her over, Eli!"

The man on the ground was having no part in the humor. The girl fought him bitterly and he yelled for help. "Gimme a hand, damn yuh!" he howled. "It'd be a purty note if'n Starke happened along now with us out here in the open."

The man on the mule had heard enough. He didn't know what to make of the inference that the pair had been waiting in ambush for Starke, but that part could come later. He spurred the mule forward so suddenly that he was in the thick of the struggle before anyone noticed him. Swinging low in the saddle, he drove in, swiftly shifting his weight in order to get full power behind the fist that he threw at Eli's jaw. The blow knocked the man completely clear of his captive and Starke followed the attack by jumping to the ground and diving upon his man. It would only be a moment until the other fellow would join the fight and Starke wanted to be sure that he was rid of one enemy before turning to face another.

After a brief but frenzied scuffle in the dust Starke had his antagonist's gun, using it as a club to batter the man to the ground again. Then he came up into a crouch to find that the girl was close beside him and directly in the path of the charging rider.

"Catch up your horse," he snapped, "and get out of here. Pronto!" He accented the words with a push that sent her sprawling out of the path of the charge. It left him just time to whirl and hack at the man who was trying to beat him down. They exchanged gun-barrel blows as the rider went past and Starke sensed that the other man would be reluctant to shoot. With that army camp just beyond the river the local thugs probably would be using a certain amount of caution.

He knew a quick sense of pain as he caught the gun barrel on the point of his shoulder, but a grunt from the horseman told him that he had hit home. Then the girl yelled, "Behind you!"

He whirled to find Eli coming back. Evidently the man had a hard head. Starke side-stepped and hammered in again with the captured gun. There was just time for Eli to gasp, "Starke! What the . . . ?" Then the gun came down and Eli collapsed. This time, Starke thought, he ought to stay put for a while.

There was no time to exult over the victory or to worry about the recognition. The other man was coming back, trying to ride Starke down. It was not the kind of tactics to be effective against a fighter reared in the rough and tumble of the border. Starke simply side-stepped the blow from his enemy's gun and yanked hard at a denim-clad leg as the horse went past. They went to the earth together, the bearded man with his face close to Starke's. He uttered a smothered curse of astonished recognition and lashed out in a frantic effort to beat down the apparent Mexican. "Yuh fooled us, damn yuh!" he panted. "Now I'm goin' to . . ."

That was as far as it went. Starke spun him with a hard left hook and followed it relentlessly with a crashing blow from Eli's gun. At a time like this there was no room for the niceties of combat; on the border you killed your enemy or disabled him before he could do the same to you.

Starke paused long enough to stare down at the faces of his fallen opponents but could find nothing familiar in either. Not that it was important; Fred Starke might have been spotted by many a man who was completely unknown to him. That was one of the penalties of being famous — or notorious. For the moment Starke didn't care too much which term he applied to himself.

He turned to where the girl was rubbing her shoulder rather gingerly. "Hurt, miss?" he asked, making no attempt to carry out his masquerade as a Mexican.

She stared curiously, frankly estimating the tall, lean young fellow who had come so surprisingly to her aid. "Mostly my temper," she said, showing white teeth in a smile that was only slightly tremulous. "Thank you very much for what you did. I didn't realize when I called that I was to be rescued by one of my own countrymen."

"Try to forget it," he said brusquely. His quick glance had told him that the girl was something of a beauty. The healthy tan of her oval features set off the tawniness of her hair, while her rumpled riding outfit made it clear that she had a most interesting figure. A man could become seriously distracted by a girl like this — and Starke couldn't afford distractions. Two days ago he would have thought that this sort of meeting would have been the perfect climax for his return to his own people, but now he was not so sure. Something was definitely wrong around San Antonio.

He glanced around and saw that her horse had broken away toward the river and was still pacing slowly. With the two thugs likely to regain consciousness at any moment, there seemed but one course of action open. He ran to where the mule had halted, vaulting into the saddle and turning the animal so vigorously that the long-ear protested with a loud bray.

"Shut up!" he said briefly. Then he leaned from the saddle to pick up the blonde girl. "We'll catch your horse and get you away from here," he explained. "Hang on and I'll see if this varmint won't hump himself a mite."

She was flustered for a moment but recovered to observe icily, "You certainly do take matters into your own hands."

He grinned into the face that was so near his own. Just now it was a sweaty, dusty face, the red of anger and violent exertion almost concealing the smoothness of the tanned skin. "Such matters I like to take into my own hands," he said quietly.

A little frown puckered her brow. "You mean . . . ?"

He pretended complete innocence. "I prefer to defend myself as best I can," he said without expression. "If I defend someone else at the same time, it is a double pleasure."

"Those men were waiting for you?"

"I think so."

"With intent to do you harm?"

He laughed. "You ask too many questions, sis. Even for as cute a gal as you are. Get ready now; we'll try to work in alongside of that bronc of yours."

"I don't like your tone."

"Stop trying to pick a fight. Nobody asked you to ride over here and stick your nose into trouble. So don't get proddy because the nose gets a mite skinned. Pay attention now; we'll be in position to grab in a minute."

Suddenly he lifted her across and dumped her into her own saddle. "Now hit the trail!" he ordered. "This ain't any country for the likes of you. Bring a squadron the next time you ride out."

For a moment it seemed that she would let her anger get the better of her. Then, surprisingly, she laughed. "I'll do that. Now tell me who you are."

"Just somebody who wanted to keep shady," he replied. "You ruined that all right. Now try to forget that you ever saw me. Meanwhile, take Eli's gun and keep it handy until you're back across the river."

"I'm sorry if I caused trouble," she said, reaching for the gun.

He gave her no opportunity to say more. As soon as she took the revolver from his fingers he whirled the mule in a short circle and sent the bewildered animal past a line of adobes and into a side lane, which seemed to lead into a more thickly populated area. He was a little ashamed that he had lost his temper in speaking to the blonde girl. Getting angry was never any good. A man had to keep his head. Anyway, a girl with so much cool nerve shouldn't get scolded for accidentally complicating a man's personal problems.

He grinned a little at his own thoughts. It was easy to forgive a pretty girl, especially when she was a sunburned blonde and a man had spent three years among Latins. Still, her intervention had not been the calamity it had first seemed. Those sentries had been watching for Fred Starke. They would have challenged any tall rider, looking for gray eyes. Merely posing as a lazy peon wouldn't have been any good. Perhaps it was good that the girl had made her move when she did. Maybe he owed her a bit of thanks.

He drove the mule hard until he had made several turns through the narrow streets of the old quarter, then he relaxed once more and picked up his pose of studied laziness. For the moment he had to strive for the old casualness, but he knew that the pose would not be good very long. Those sentinels would be regaining their senses and reporting back to the man who had put them on watch.

At a stable, where a fat Mexican was just beginning to stir after his siesta, Starke halted and put through a fast dicker. A bit of gold and the tired mule brought him a chestnut mustang that looked mean but was of sturdy build. Riding a bronc might help to fool men who would now be looking for a mule-rider.

A quarter of a mile farther along he entered a store which carried secondhand clothing, as well as hardware and other odds and ends. There he bought a felt hat which he suspected had once been army property. Carrying it under his arm, he moved on until he found a spot where he could change clothing unobserved. The huge sombrero went behind some bushes and the campaign hat took its place. A flannel shirt from a saddlebag replaced the lighter garment he had been wearing. A heavy belt took the place of the sash. When he rode on he was no longer a sleepy Mexican. Instead, he appeared to be a young Texan fresh in from a ranch.

A slow circle of the district permitted him to check his back trail and to make certain that no one was following him. Dusk was beginning to fall by that time and he knew a feeling of some relief. The worst of the immediate danger was over. Now he had only to make a contact with Diego before pushing on to the army camp to make his report.

Straighter in the saddle now, for all his air of carelessness, he looked much taller than the Mexican who had slept his way in from the south an hour earlier. It was a risk to appear so much like himself, he knew, but under the circumstances it was the best he could do.

Darkness was falling heavily upon the Mexican quarter when he found the spot he sought, a cantina which seemed to be well patronized and was almost too well lighted. Starke knew a feeling of regret that Diego had not picked a less public meeting place, but he hesitated only briefly before tying the bronc at the hitching rack and going in. Perhaps the place would be safe enough; certainly Diego wouldn't make his headquarters at any spot except where friends would be available.

The interior was quite spacious under its low ceiling. Most of the customers were at the bar, which ran across the short side of the room, but a few were already engaged with suppers that had been served to them at small tables along the bare walls. The open space in the

12

middle was clearly reserved for dancing, which would be a part of a later program.

Starke went to a table without even looking toward the bar. He kept his sombrero on when he sat down, using it to shade his face as much as possible. A sidelong glance told him that Diego was not in the room and he wondered how long he would have to risk discovery before meeting his friend. While he was thinking about it, there was a quick tap of heels at his side and he looked up into the largest black eyes he had ever seen. The eyes were set in an olive-skinned oval face that was almost flawless in its dark beauty.

"The *señor* wishes supper?" the girl asked, her English almost without accent. The little frown, which went as swiftly as it had come, told him that she was curious about him, probably because she had been tipped off to expect him. He was about to give her a sign of recognition when he realized that two men at the bar had turned to watch him. Both were Americans.

"Sure," he growled, letting the drawl take on a thickness that would conceal his normal tones. "Supper it is, kid. Anything that ain't too full o' Mex peppers. I ain't made o' iron inside."

"Chili?" she asked, faltering a little.

"Anything at all," he growled. "I dunno much about yuhr kind o' grub. Jest hustle it up."

CHAPTER
TWO

The girl paused only a moment, turning away without a word and hurrying through an open doorway which evidently led to the kitchen. Starke felt certain that she had expected him and had recognized him. That part was all right, but he didn't propose to make any move until he was more certain of his surroundings. Those two men at the bar were a trifle too interested.

He eased back in his chair, assuming an air of apathy. The move permitted him to slide an elbow across his middle and loosen the gun he had shoved into the waistband of his pants. There was a chance he might need it and he didn't want it to be stuck.

Presently he stretched and turned his head to look around the room with lazy nonchalance. He saw five Mexicans eating supper at the tables along the wall and six others ranged along the bar. The two Americans at the bar held slightly aloof, nursing generous glasses of tequila. Back of the bar a lean Mexican with a sweeping black mustache was serving his customers briskly. For such an early hour the cantina seemed to be doing good business.

Starke showed no sign of interest in any part of it, settling back a little lower in his chair as if sinking more deeply into his boredom. The two Americans were talking in whispers now and he had a hunch that their conversation was about him. His new position permitted him to watch them from beneath drooping eyelids.

The pair of them came across the room then, halting close beside him. He had already appraised them to himself and decided they were hard cases. One was clean-shaven except for bushy sideburns, while the other sported a mustache and an imperial. Otherwise, they vaguely resembled each other, both being sandy in complexion, of medium height, and slightly on the pudgy side. Both had regular features with no particular marks of distinction, and both wore guns hung low over right hips.

Starke didn't move even when they halted within easy reach of him. He was conscious of the hard shape of the gun against his belly, but he did not let a hand stray toward it. He was still apparently half asleep when the man with the sideburns snapped, "Wake up there, partner! Seems like us Gringos oughta git together. Come over and swill a bit o' tarantula juice with us."

He laughed as he uttered the invitation, but the sound was not convincing. The humor had been a little too forced and the man was not enough of an actor to hide the tension back of his offer. Starke read the warning and managed to look particularly stupid as he squinted upward. "I had more'n I need now, brother," he drawled, exaggerating the accent until he hoped it would cover the intonation which he had never been

15

able to hide entirely. "Sorry, but I'm aimin' to git me some vittles fust."

"Yuh're plumb unfriendly," the second man stated flatly. "We ain't a-likin' it."

"Nossir," Sideburns declared. "When we ask a man to drink with us we ain't a-takin' no fer a answer."

Starke still did not make a move. He understood the strategy well enough. This pair was on watch for a man who had been described to them. They wanted to see the eyes of any stranger who was not definitely a Mexican. Their first bit of strategy had failed, so now they were trying to goad him into the move they wanted. He was curious to see how far they would go. More than that, he wanted to let them talk, hoping that they would let something slip. It might be very important to know who was setting up this cordon of sentinels around San Antonio.

Then one of the men made a mistake. He grabbed Starke by the shoulder as though to shake him into attention. Instantly Starke threw off the hand, whirling in the same motion to bring himself out of his chair and to draw the gun from his waistband. Before either of the strangers quite knew what had happened, they were facing the menacing barrel of a Colt .44 revolver. Still hoping to keep his eyes from being too plainly seen, Starke glared through narrowed lids; in his whole attitude was a cold threat which the pair seemed to recognize.

"I ain't drinkin', understand?" he growled, again putting something extra into his voice as a disguise. "And don't come around here with none o' yer

16

rawhidin', yuh stinkin' polecats. I ain't no greenhorn Yankee. Now git!" The final order was fairly explosive and he punctuated it by taking a step toward them, jabbing suggestively with the six-gun.

From the bar a mixed torrent of English and Spanish pleaded with the *señores* not to start anything that would bring trouble upon the house. Starke made up his mind quickly. If this cantina was the spot which was to be used for his contacts with Diego, he could not afford to make it look like a suspicious spot.

"I'm gittin' outa here," he snarled, edging around the two men, who stood motionless in the middle of the floor. "And don't neither o' yuh try to foller me till I've got me a good start. Yuh'll meet lead if'n yuh come out too soon." He let the gun waver only enough to suggest that he was watching every man in the room, not merely the two in front of him. There was a flat silence as he sidled swiftly toward the door, and then he was out in the night, mounting his horse and riding away with enough clatter to suggest that he intended to put plenty of miles behind him in a hurry.

He kept the bronc at a gallop until he had rounded the first corner, but then he eased down and made another sharp turn, cutting back toward the cantina through what appeared to be some sort of alley. There were a few shacks along it, but mostly they appeared to be sheds rather than dwellings. None were lighted, and he dismounted as he closed in on the rear of the place he had recently left, satisfied that there had been no immediate pursuit.

A convenient cabbage palm provided a place to tie the horse and within another minute or two he was moving silently toward the lighted kitchen windows of the cantina. It was then that a soft voice spoke almost in his ear. "A worthy bit of strategy, my friend. For a moment we feared that you would do something hasty and call attention down upon our little retreat." The sibilant English was just a little too perfect to be coming from an Anglo-Saxon.

"You scared me, Diego," Starke grunted. "Were you inside when I had my little fracas?"

The shadow beside him was as tall as himself. "Of a certainty, companero. But not in the main room, of course. I remained out of sight since the hour when the enemy posted his guard. Unhappily for me I expected to see you in Mexican garb and was caught off guard by your actual appearance."

"Then the two Americans in there were really looking for me?"

"Of a certainty. Others are in the town doing the same thing. At first we feared that our rendezvous had been discovered. Now it appears that they merely post many guards."

"Who's doing all this?" Starke asked. "I ran into a couple of men a while ago. Who's so anxious to stop me — and who was so sure that I'd be along?"

"Come," Diego said softly. "We talk where it is safer. There is much to be said."

"My horse. We can't leave him out here to be spotted."

"Pablo will put him in the stable. Come."

18

He led the way to a small building adjoining the cantina. No light appeared in it, but two dark shadows along its wall indicated that it was not abandoned. Diego spoke in Spanish now, issuing quick orders to the men who had been waiting there. In return he was informed that the two *Americanos* still lingered in the cantina. Evidently they did not yet realize that their quarry had slipped through their fingers.

"You can trust these men completely?" Starke asked when the two Mexicans melted into the shadows.

"Enough," Diego told him. "Pablo and Felipe are the sons of old Manuel who owns the cantina. That was Manuel at the bar. The girl Lirio is his daughter. Along with old Maria the cook, they are my staff. Loyal Juaristas every one. Grope along the right hand wall and you will find a settee."

Starke followed directions, content to accept Diego's reply. In the three years of his acquaintanceship with the Juarez lieutenant, he had never found any reason to doubt the man's honesty or judgment. If Diego said these people were safe, that was good enough for Fred Starke.

They were seated together on what felt like a wooden bench before either man spoke again. Then Starke asked bluntly, "What's happened to the plans?"

"Whose plans?" Diego countered.

Starke wiped sweat from his forehead. The evening had cooled but little and the atmosphere inside of this house was still much too warm for comfort. The darkness was heavy, almost oppressive. "I'm a little puzzled," he said slowly. "I expected to drift in here today and be welcomed as a sort of returning prodigal. I had visions of a kind of security haven't known for over three years. Instead of being on my own, alert against every sound and movement, I was going to be in a camp of the United States army, a camp of victorious veterans who would provide me with absolute safety." He laughed harshly as he added, "And now I can't even reach that camp without running a gantlet. What has happened around here anyway?"

"Several things," Diego said soberly. "Things I do not like. You heard that General Sheridan has been ordered to withhold aid to our gallant Juarez?"

"No! When did this happen? The last I heard was that Sheridan was going to support Juarez to the full extent of the fifty thousand-man force he was moving down into the border country. Who changed the orders?"

"Your country's State Department, I understand. The devious paths of diplomacy are to be followed first. Louis Napoleon has been given to understand that the United States considers his support of Maximilian to be a violation of the Monroe Doctrine. Sheridan's army moves to the border as a bit of emphasis behind the statement, but no actual violation of neutrality is to be permitted. Napoleon is to be given no excuse to claim that your country has interfered in the affairs of Mexico."

"But what of the help Sheridan promised to Juarez?"

"I would greatly like to know the answer to that question."

"I'd prefer to know who these people are that are so anxious to keep me from reaching the army camp."

"On that I am better informed. You undoubtedly know that the surrender of the Confederacy left several thousand rebel soldiers at loose ends in this country. Many have never actually surrendered. Some have enlisted with Maximilian's other mercenaries in my own unhappy country. Others operate as guerrillas, hoping that the unsettled conditions here will offer them an opportunity for plunder."

"But what do they want of me?"

"Vengeance, perhaps. Maximilian tried to help the Confederacy with supplies during your war. You were the gadfly who pestered both sides. Their alliance is still in some sort of operation and it would be quite satisfactory to both groups of our enemies if they could do something about you."

"Then renegade Texans are actually preparing to help the Maximilian government to maintain itself in Mexico?"

"Of a certainty. They have little cause to feel kindly toward your Federal government. Now they can indulge their ill humor by being spiteful — and perhaps take a fee for so doing. It is not beyond the range of imagination to think that Maximilian and his hirelings will pay for guerrilla activities on this side of the border as well as for formal service south of the Rio Grande."

Starke grunted his understanding of the situation. After battling the combined forces of Confederates and Mexican Imperials for three years, he understood how these oddly assorted allies might still stick together.

21

Defeated Texans might hope to gain some advantage for themselves by helping to keep Maximilian on the throne of Mexico.

"How many of 'em have joined Maximilian?" Starke asked.

He could almost feel Diego's shrug in the hot gloom. "*Quien sabe?*" the Mexican murmured. "Some say no more than three hundred, some say five thousand. Many do not enlist openly but remain on this side of the border to operate secretly when the time comes for action."

"Does our command know this?"

"I think not. It is one reason why you should not delay in reporting to General Merritt. He is the one who commands here."

Starke laughed harshly. "I wonder if he'll believe what I tell him? All the evidence seems to indicate that our military authorities don't even know that I exist. Certainly I've had neither pay nor promotion after three years of rather strenuous service."

"You explained that yourself long ago," Diego retorted. "Your orders have been secret, never from your army. Someone will know about you, I'm sure. Three years of raiding those supply trains along the Rio Grande will not have gone unnoticed."

"Don't butter me up, Diego. I know how the army works. The fellow who gets the promotions is the lad who's placed where somebody can see him."

"You do not talk like Serranias Starke now," Diego said with a chuckle. "Our Coahuila raiders would not recognize you in such a mood."

22

His humor got a quick response. "Self-pity," Starke said shortly. "A bad habit to get into. Maybe I'm just extra-apprehensive because I'm disappointed to find that the army hasn't got everything under control."

"On that point you are quite correct. They mistake the collapse of the Confederacy for a collapse of rebel sentiment."

"Then there's a connection between the Mexican alliance and some new rebellion?"

"I think so. Texans obviously hope to draw pay from Maximilian and at the same time profit by looting supply trains sent by the United States for the use of Juarez. There is even talk that some former rebels hope to transfer the Confederacy to Mexico, either by working with Maximilian or by betraying him. In any event, it would seem that we are in for a very bad time along the Rio Grande."

"Who are the leaders?" Starke asked. "If I'm going to take information to General Merritt, I might as well have it as complete as possible."

"I call them the Floral Boys," Diego said solemnly. "Undoubtedly that is a bit of misguided humor, probably due to my long residence among American wits. The principal civilian agent is a fellow named Rose, while the most important military commander is a Captain Lily, formerly commander of a body of Rebel irregulars. You know Lily, I believe."

Diego did not need to say more. He knew Starke well enough to realize what the name Lily meant to him. The outlaw leader had dropped out of sight toward the end of the war, disowned by the Confederate government. His reappearance in a position of authority branded the new development as something pretty deadly. If Miles Lily was in it, there would be nothing decent or ethical in any part of it.

"Rose and Lily," Starke murmured thoughtfully. "I suppose it's a proper moment to quote something about a rose by any other name being just as deadly. Or did your favorite author Cervantes say something more to the point?"

Diego's laugh was rather perfunctory. "You never fail to taunt me about my predilection for literary phrases. Please take note that in the present circumstances I have little heart for cultural matters." He chuckled again and added, "If you insist on a quotation for old time's sake, however, I recall one from Reginald Heber. 'Death rides on every passing breeze, he lurks in every flower.' That takes care of both Rose and Lily. They're a bad pair."

"I'll watch out for 'em," Starke promised. "However, I can do a quote on that matter myself. Don't ask me who said it; I'm not the scholar you are. It just runs something like, 'Leaves have their time to fall, and flowers to wither.' Maybe we're due to give Lily and Rose a little of what is coming to them."

"Quotation from Hemans," Diego said quietly. "Very appropriate, too, since the rest of it is ' . . . at the north wind's breath.' We'll hope this Northern army is going to take a good fall out of the pair in question."

"Meanwhile I'll watch. But what about other facts which may be of use to our forces? Anything I can take along with me will be that much help to us later. Fill me in on any details you think may be useful."

Diego talked steadily for five minutes, giving Starke complete details on the strength of the Imperial forces in Mexico. He was interrupted by a voice at the door.

"The Americans have gone," the voice stated quietly in Spanish. "A messenger came and ordered them to join a picket line beyond the river. This much but no more my father overheard."

"Well done, Pablo," Diego told him. "It is time to move."

"Any names mentioned?" Starke asked, using Spanish that was as fluent as that of the Mexicans.

"No, señor. Only what I have said."

"They're throwing guards around the whole camp, I think," Diego said quietly. "That gives you some idea of how many men they are able to call into service. Come. We walk and tell you about how you will find the camp of the General Staff. You must be careful; there are many small camps making up the large ones, and enemies may lurk between. Leave your horse here for the present."

"You think I should go on tonight?"

"'Delay always breeds danger,'" Diego stated firmly. "That, in case you do not recognize it, is a quotation from Cervantes."

Starke chuckled. "Let's go. When Diego Menendez and Cervantes team up on me I surrender."

"Anyway, it is well to move by dark," Diego added. "By day you are too easily recognized."

They were silent as they went out into the street and headed north. For the moment neither cared to continue the banter and neither felt any need to talk. It was better to keep quiet and stay alert.

At length Diego spoke again. "Sorry you had to miss supper," he said as they strolled casually through the cleaner part of the Mexican district. "We'll pick up a snack later if everything seems clear."

"I've missed meals before," Starke told him. "I was more interested in that gal with the big eyes. She's worth a couple of extra looks."

"I know. I do the looking."

"Sorry. I didn't know you'd staked a claim."

Diego waved his long cigar airily, keeping his voice low but putting on a good show of being the genial man-about-town talking to a fellow gossip. "No harm done. I mix business with pleasure. Old Manuel and his sons are most valuable to our cause. The fair Lirio can be even more useful — as well as most ornamental."

"Then you better get back. If I was on cozy terms with a gal like that one I wouldn't go tramping around San Antonio with any bullet bait like me."

"It is safer with two," Diego told him. "They look for one man. I will point out the part of the camp you should approach; then I leave you."

They crossed the river without challenge and presently found themselves on a sort of ridge from which the sprawling campfires of the army could be seen clearly. Diego muttered a few directions and shook Starke's hand. "I'll keep in touch," he promised. "Your success will be mine, you know."

Then he was gone into the night, and Starke found himself moving into a stretch of rough country which he knew would almost certainly be under patrol by the enemy.

CHAPTER
THREE

Starke found it difficult to fight down the feeling that this was all some sort of crazy dream. For weeks he had been anticipating his return to a more normal relationship with the army, but always he had thought of that army as a conquering force, the army that had broken the power of the Confederacy. More recently he had thought of it as the army that would drive the French invaders out of Mexico. Now he was having to sneak into its camp, risking his life on his own ability to dodge enemies that the army didn't even know it had. The situation would have been ridiculous if it hadn't been so dangerous.

He moved as silently as his border training required, catching now and then a flicker of light from the sprawling encampment as he slipped across the top of a ridge. Never did he pause to study the scene ahead; a scout didn't spend unnecessary minutes on the tops of ridges. Not if he expected to remain alive.

His progress was slow, as he took all proper precautions, but it was not long before he realized that the lines of campfires were not very far ahead. Either he had slipped through the enemy lines or they were playing it boldly, posting their sentries almost within speaking distance of the army picket line.

A soft scuff of a foot warned him that the latter guess was the correct one. Evidently the guerrilla leaders were taking full advantage of the army's complacency. Starke listened and then moved forward again, the habits of three dangerous years turning him into something that was almost Indian. He worked his way through some dry mesquite, taking infinite pains that no dry branch would crackle. Twice more he heard the footsteps, and the second time he was close enough to make out the form of a man waiting silently beneath a small cabbage palm.

For a good five minutes he held his position, watching and listening. Then another footfall sounded and the man beneath the palm challenged sharply but in a hoarse whisper. He was answered promptly, both sets of words coming clearly enough to Starke. The second man simply said, "It's Mac. Don't git hasty with that trigger." Evidently the guards were under orders to shoot without delay. If one of their group could manage to ambush and murder Fred Starke it would be a simple matter for the rest of the sentry line to fade away in the darkness.

Starke risked a move as the pair closed in on each other, letting the sound of their movements cover any rustle he might make. As a result he was within a dozen feet of them when they stood together in the shadow of the palm.

The man who had identified himself as Mac asked, "Yuh sure yuh ain't let him slip past? This is the easy road fer him, yuh know. It's the way he's most likely to come."

"That's jest how come he won't use it," the other scoffed.

"Starke ain't no greenhorn. For three years he's been doin' jest what nobody figgered him to do. That's how come he's still alive."

"He'll slip sooner or later."

"Not this much. Yuh better jest trot along and stir up some o' the boys in the unlikely spots. He won't pass here. If'n he does, I know what to do."

"That's what I'm out to see. Repeat yer orders."

"Gettin' damn important, ain't yuh, Mac? Sounds like yuh think we're back in Kirby Smith's army."

"Mebbe it'll come to that," the other said darkly. "Repeat them orders and quit sulkin'."

"All right. Don't git so proddy. If'n anybody comes by here I'm to make out I'm a drunken Mex. I git him close enough to make sure it's Starke, and if'n he is, I stick a knife into him. If'n I can't git him close but I'm sure it's Starke, I shoot him and git."

"Right. Jest keep them orders in mind. No shootin' if yuh kin avoid it — but don't forget who yuh're dealin' with. Yuh won't live to make no mistakes."

"Trust me. How near's our next man?"

"Fifty yards, more or less. We're stringin' 'em mighty close along here."

Starke listened while the guard officer moved along into the west. He had hoped to learn a little more about the identity of his enemies, but the talk between the two men had merely corroborated the statements Diego had made. A substantial force of former rebels had turned into a guerrilla army. That force was out to kill Fred Starke. Maybe they wanted him out of the way before they started some sort of project; maybe they simply wanted revenge for the defeats he had thrust upon them along the border. For the moment their reason was not important.

No Comanche ever moved more silently than Starke as he circled to move in behind the sentry. It took a good ten minutes to cover the short distance, but finally Starke was within reaching range, drawing his gun. Even that motion was one of the utmost patience. The weapon came out slowly, each move calculated to reduce the risk of a betraying rustle. Suddenly the gun was clear, and Starke discarded caution for speed. The gun swung in a vicious arc, its barrel crashing down upon the head of the unsuspecting sentry. There was the thud of the blow, a wheezing sort of grunt as the man went down, and then Starke was standing over him, a grim smile crinkling his lips in the darkness. Going to knife me, are you? he gritted to himself.

He listened for a moment to make sure that the sound of the blow and the fall had not aroused anyone else. The night was silent except for the murmur of sound from the army camp. Starke leaned over to search the guard's pockets but found nothing of significance. Then he turned and moved quickly toward the last ridge that blocked his view of the encampment.

It was easy enough after that. He passed through the sentry line of the army camp without even a formal challenge. A blue-coated infantryman stopped his pacing long enough to say "Hi!" but it was more of a social gesture than anything else. Starke replied in much the same tone, but he did not like to see matters going like that. It was time the military authorities learned that this expedition to southern Texas wasn't going to be a picnic.

He made no inquiries until he was well within the camp itself, preferring to get away from the edge of the encampment before taking time for anything. The men who had been out to get him might even risk firing into the camp if they thought they could pick him off and get away with it.

He strode casually along between the orderly rows of pale tents, trying to stifle the feeling of nostalgia that came over him. He had known this kind of military life just long enough for it to have done something to him. After three years of enforced absence from it he scarcely knew how to accept the change. Company streets, guard details, cooking fires, all the orderly aspects of military life were there, but now they didn't seem so familiar. Nothing was new; it simply was not what Fred Starke had come to accept as his normal outlook.

Men lounged around fires or tent flaps as the coolness of the evening came to dispel that dry heat of the afternoon. Here and there an officer in shirt sleeves would show himself briefly, but no one seemed at all disposed to take anything seriously, not even the stranger who wandered unchallenged through the camp.

Finally Starke accosted an infantryman who leaned on his musket in front of what seemed to be some sort of company headquarters tent. "Evenin', soldier. Got any idea where I might locate a Colonel Haney of General Merritt's staff?"

The bluecoat shrugged wearily. "I dunno about this here Colonel Haney, mister, but the General's headquarters is down thataway a piece. Mebbe a quarter mile or so. You can't miss it. They'll be actin' real busy down there." He jerked a thumb over his right shoulder as he spoke.

"That'll mark it for sure," Starke told him easily. He walked on, studying regimental insignia wherever he could spot them. Before long he could make a pretty good estimate of the nature and number of troops in the camp. Merritt must have about five thousand in camp, not counting teamsters and other camp followers. Of the number more than half seemed to be cavalry. That was good. Infantry wouldn't amount to much here on the border.

Not so cheering was the sight of several companies of colored troops. During the war nothing had enraged the Confederates more than having Negro troops used against them. Starke felt pretty certain that the use of such troopers in the occupation force would be likely to cause plenty of hard feeling. If the government in Washington hoped to get Southern support for the demonstration against Mexico, they were certainly going about it in the wrong fashion.

A couple of inquiries gave him all the help he needed and within a matter of minutes he was standing at the open end of a large tent. There was no sentry on duty and for a moment he wondered if he had come to the wrong place. An officer like Colonel Haney should at least have an orderly on duty. Then he saw the two men who had been seated just beyond a swinging lantern. One appeared to be quite young, while the other was a nondescript individual in his late forties. Neither wore enough uniform to show rank, but the younger and larger man showed the broad yellow stripe of the cavalry on the seams of his riding breeches.

"Is this Colonel Haney's quarters?" Starke asked abruptly.

The younger man's face showed something like irritation at the query, but the older one merely nodded, no emotion showing at all. He was the sort of person who would be unnoticed in almost any kind of gathering, a man of medium height, medium build and medium complexion. "I'm Haney," he declared in a voice as colorless as his person.

"I'm Fred Starke," the newcomer stated. "From across the border. Orders delivered through Captain Gauntt."

"Starke, eh?" the flat voice commented. "You have the word?"

"Yes, sir. It is Mississippi."

"Correct. And your orders were issued by whom?"

"Colonel Sebring — sir." He had to add the sir after a perceptible pause. Three years made a man forget his old habits.

"One more question. Your last order before this one was issued by whom?"

"The officer in charge of undercover information. I never knew his name. That was in September of 1862. I've been carrying out those orders ever since."

"I guess you're Starke, all right," Haney said. "Come in and take a seat on that box beside Ritchie. This is Captain Ritchie, formerly of the headquarters troop of the Ninth Cavalry. At present he is assigned to this project. You might as well get acquainted with him now; you'll be working together."

Starke shook hands with the big man. So far he liked what had happened. Colonel Haney showed signs of knowing his business and he wasn't making any fuss about rank or show. Even his appearance hinted that he was accustomed to working quietly and in the dark, something that could not be said about every undercover information officer.

"What is the project you mention, sir?" Starke asked when he was seated. "My orders hinted that our force was preparing to move aid to Juarez and that I was expected to help with it. Beyond that I have no information."

"You ask questions in a hurry, mister," Captain Ritchie growled. "How can we be sure that you're really Starke and not some guerrilla trying to get information?"

"I thought the matter of the password was supposed to settle it."

"Not for me. There must be a lot of people in the border country who know a few things about Starke and who might have picked up information about the orders Gauntt carried."

"Reasonable," Starke agreed. "I won't complain. All through camp I've been making mental criticisms of the army's laxity. Now I'll have to agree that you're not making the same mistake. What can I do to identify myself?"

"I'm satisfied," Colonel Haney said quietly.

"I'm not," the younger man persisted. "With your permission, sir, I'd like to check up a bit more."

When no one spoke, he swung to face Starke once more. "We'll skip the parts that everyone knows. Lieutenant Starke was somehow stranded in Texas when the rebellion broke out. He couldn't rejoin the Federal forces but went to Mexico instead. There he received orders to organize a band of border raiders and to check the flow of European supplies that were coming into the Confederacy through Mexico. That part is known to a great many people, so it will be meaningless for our purpose. Suppose you tell me your story prior to the war. I know enough about it to judge its truth."

Starke had to grin a little at the other man's stern manner. He had a feeling that young Captain Ritchie was taking himself pretty seriously, but he had to admit that in the present circumstances it was rather a good idea.

"I'll outline it. If you want to ask about details fire away. I came out of West Point in 1859 and was assigned to border patrol down here in my home state. I was lucky on my first assignment, catching some Comanche raiders and drawing a quick promotion. My only one, I might add. The War Department seems to have forgotten me completely. However, that's beside the point. I was along the Rio Grande when secessionism boiled up. Our company was split just as the southern states were. Our captain resigned and joined the Confederate army. The other lieutenants disappeared, probably for the same reason. About half of the men deserted. I was left with a handful of loyal men and no instructions."

"You were no more confused than the rest of us," Colonel Haney said. "It was happening everywhere. No one knew what to do."

Starke nodded. "I decided to put it up to Governor Sam Houston. He was an old friend of my family and had gotten me my appointment to the Academy when he was in Congress. I left my men in camp and headed up to Austin to see him. By the time I got there the state had joined the Confederacy in spite of his efforts, and he had resigned rather than be a part of such a move.

"The news of Fort Sumter came through just then and I was in a bad spot. I couldn't do anything but make an attempt to get back to my men and slip away into Mexico. That attempt was doomed almost immediately. I met some other Unionists who were aiming for the Rio Grande, but we ran afoul of a guerrilla outfit and in the skirmish I was wounded."

"When did this happen?" Ritchie asked sharply.

"May of 1861."

"Go on." There was real suspicion in the big fellow's tone now.

Starke chuckled a little. "I'll bet you've heard about the fight on the Nueces and think you've got me in a lie. Let me tell you the rest of it. I laid up with a loyal German family all during that summer. They had come over here to live in a *United* States and they didn't like the idea of having the country divided. They had to keep quiet about their sentiments, but they took good care of me while I was getting back on my feet."

"We heard that there was a sort of Terror down here during that period," Haney said. "Was it really so bad?"

"Bad enough. Wise and Denton Counties had a whole series of lynchings. Armed thugs patrolled the country, stringing up any folks who sounded at all sympathetic to the Union. Partly because of them and partly because of my wounds, I didn't try to get away until the following spring. Then I joined a band of young fellows, mostly from German families, who had decided to get through to the Union forces around New Orleans. The plan was to move south into Mexico and then find passage on a Union patrol vessel.

"We did well enough until we were ambushed by a guerrilla crowd under a couple of real cut-throats. Captain Duff and Lieutenant Lily were their names. I was wounded again but managed to get away. About a third of our boys were killed before they would surrender, and then the guerrillas shot most of their prisoners anyway."

"What was the date of this?" Ritchie snapped.

"August ninth, 1862. I managed to get away into Mexico in spite of my wound and was again taken in by some mighty fine people, this time a family of Juarez sympathizers who had been driven from their homes by Clericals. They got in touch with our nearest consul and it was through him that I eventually received orders to stay where I was and make plans to harass supply trains traveling into Texas."

"One more question," Ritchie said, a little less sternly. "How many supply trains did you claim to have destroyed? As of your last report, I mean."

Starke laughed aloud. "I've never made a report."

A dry chuckle came from Colonel Haney. "I guess we'll take you on trust now, Starke. But while you're at it you might as well tell us the rest. We're interested, you know. Did you work with the Juarez forces while you operated down there?"

"Most of the time. I had to have men who would risk their lives and Juarez supporters were the logical ones. They were willing to take a crack at the French or the Imperials who convoyed the shipments north to the border."

"Didn't Napoleon's veterans make trouble for you after they came into the picture?"

"They tried, but Europeans are not much good at our kind of warfare. That was why we generally staged our raids south of the border. We could outwit Maximilian's parade soldiers a lot easier, and we had less distance to haul the loot after we got it. Stealing the material was of great importance to my men, as you doubtless realize."

"I'll ask my question in a different way," Captain Ritchie put in. "How many trains did you capture altogether?"

"We got clean away with an even dozen, taking wagons and all back into the Serranias del Burro, the mountain region of Coahuila where we holed up between raids. Mostly we settled for two or three wagons out of each train, burning the rest and getting away fast. I suppose we destroyed seven or eight hundred wagons and got away with perhaps a hundred more in addition to the twelve full trains."

Ritchie whistled. "No wonder we heard that they put a price on your head. You must have kept them in a dither."

"I tried," Starke said shortly.

Colonel Haney chuckled again. "You're willing to accept him for what he claims, Captain?"

Ritchie nodded, a grin spreading across his broad features. "I guess I was too doubting. He's Starke, right enough."

"Good. Now let's get down to business. We'll swap information right away, and then we'll know what kind of moves to make in the morning. All right with you, Starke?"

"That's why I'm here, sir. You call the shots."

CHAPTER
FOUR

There was a moment or two of silence in the semi-gloom, but then Colonel Haney began to talk. Evidently he had decided to accept Starke without reservation and was anxious to pass on the information. "I may repeat what you already know," he began, "but I think it will be well to fill you in completely.

"It was an open secret that we came down here to help Juarez get back into office as president of Mexico. General Sheridan made a couple of speeches about the Maximilian government being piratical and even sent Captain Gauntt to contact the Juarez forces. Then our orders were changed abruptly. We are not to make any overt move against the international border. We are supposed to be darkly threatening, but we must not make any first move. France must have a good opportunity to take the hint and get out. Meanwhile, we are to use every means short of open action to make that hint stronger."

"Then we still intend to support Juarez, sir?" Starke asked.

"Evidently so. He is still the legally elected head of Mexico. Supporting him is both logical and legal. But we're not ready to make an open move until we see if a huge bluff won't work. The ticklish part will be to put teeth into the bluff without actually biting anybody. That's why we wanted you."

"How many people knew that I was due here?" Starke inquired. "I ask the question because it seems pretty certain that a lot of folks had ideas about stopping me."

"What makes you think so?"

Starke told his story in short form, omitting any mention of the blonde girl. "No mistake about it," he concluded. "In each case I heard enough to know that I was the one they were after."

"You mean there is a rebel force of that size operating here?" Haney did not try to hide his astonishment.

"Big enough to picket this camp, apparently."

"Any idea why they want to catch you?"

"There's the reward offered by the Mexican Imperials, of course. It could be that."

"You don't seem too certain."

"I'm not. You see, I've been informed that the principal leaders of this *sub rosa* army are a couple of men named Rose and Lily respectively. Miles Lily is the same Lieutenant Lily who commanded that gang of butchers who massacred the German lads. I know Rose only by reputation, but he has not had much Mexican background. My guess is that they have something else than a reward in mind."

"And I think you're right. Try this one on for size. The Mexicans know that you have been called back for reassignment. They know that you will be used in

42

making contact with the Juarez forces. They know that you will learn the exact nature of our intentions. They also know that you are a stranger to all of us in this force. At least I'm guessing that their sources of information will have made those points clear to them. So they try to intercept you, planning to substitute an agent of their own who will pose as you and thus learn what we intend to do."

"It's an idea, sir," Starke admitted. "It lets me down a little. I was flattering myself that they must hate me a lot to try so hard to get me. Now it would seem that they just wanted to eliminate me as a means of getting a spy into camp."

"You almost sound annoyed."

"I'm really relieved. This camp is mighty easy for a stranger to enter. I wasn't feeling any too safe about being here. Now maybe I won't be so skittish."

"You say you know Rose by reputation. Will you explain that?"

"Of course. He was the agent who tried to salvage something out of the Confederacy. Some fifteen thousand die-hards were camped around Marshall when word of the surrender came and they refused to disband. We heard a rumor that they planned to invade Mexico with the idea of re-establishing the Confederacy there. Then they must have changed their minds, for Rose acted as their envoy and offered to enlist the whole outfit in Maximilian's army. It looks like some of that force must have been ordered to stay here and pose as civilians."

"You think they're in the pay of the Maximilian government?"

"Maybe. More likely they're trying to draw pay from Max and at the same time figure to do some looting on their own."

"Guessing?" Ritchie asked, his tone curt.

"Guessing," Starke agreed. "Of course there's some basis for the guesswork. A lot of Johnny Rebs went across the border in violation of surrender terms, so it's reasonable to suppose that the ones on this side aren't any more to be trusted."

"We're trying to get the facts on that," Haney said quickly. "How much can you tell us about the men who violated the surrender?"

"Not very much, I'm afraid. At least not much that General Sheridan doesn't already know. After Kirby Smith surrendered to General Canby in May, he didn't make any attempt to keep his men from slipping away in violation of parole. Maybe three thousand of them went south and enlisted with Maximilian. Some of them went as units under leaders like Shelby, Magruder, Slaughter, and Walker. They took artillery, ammunition, and stores with them."

"You're sure of this?"

Starke grinned slightly. "It's just a report — but I reckon General Sheridan believes it. At any rate, I heard this afternoon that he was making real nasty noises at old Mejia, the Mex commander in Coahuila, demanding that Mejia send back the stuff that was taken across the border in violation of surrender terms.

The rumor also says that Mejia is going to be a good boy and send the stuff back."

The older officer didn't seem to be very happy over that piece of information, probably, Starke thought, because he had been kept in the dark about it. Then he brightened a little. "If they're willing to meet our demands it would seem that they're not planning to cause an open break."

"Either that or they're not ready yet."

"We'll guess on that point later. Just now the important matter is to get on with plans. We must help Juarez without committing ourselves to any violation of the border. That means smuggling guns and ammunition to him so as to build up his strength to a point where he'll be able to strike hard when the time comes for us to stop pettifogging. That's where you come in. You're the fellow who's going to run the guns."

"Sounds interesting. All I have to do is haul a few guns back into the Mexican hills while the Imperial army, the United States Department of State, a couple of thousand Texas guerrillas, and some assorted Lipans and Comanches try to stop me. If I'm real lucky, the United States army will stay neutral and not interfere."

"No point in getting sarcastic, mister," Ritchie snapped.

"Maybe you've been on detached duty long enough to forget that orders are orders in this army."

"Easy," Haney cautioned. "We're not issuing orders to Lieutenant Starke. The things we're asking him to do are not a matter for orders."

"Maybe we'd better have his status explained," Ritchie suggested stiffly. "When you informed me that Mr. Starke would be attached to my company, I understood that he was to be a part of the command. If he is to be a guest, not subject to orders, I think I should know."

Haney laughed uneasily. "You've been around Major Mallory too long, Captain. Don't set so blessed much store by military rank." He turned to aim his next remark at Starke, clearly a bit troubled by the turn matters had taken. "We'd planned to have you become just another officer in the camp, Starke. The anonymity of numbers, you know. If you were just another junior officer on routine duty, there would not be so much chance of gossip starting."

"Sounds like a good idea, sir," Starke told him, steadily. "It might even be protective coloration for me. I'm still not certain that the various attempts on my life might not be repeated. I'll be harder for my enemies to find if I'm not conspicuous."

"Then you won't mind becoming a part of Captain Ritchie's detachment?" He asked the question half apologetically.

Ritchie snorted angrily, but Starke ignored him. "It sounds like a good idea, sir. If I can be provided with a uniform, I should be a bit harder for the enemy to find. Will the plan to get these supplies to Juarez go forward without delay?"

"Just as soon as we can get the facts on the situation you outline. I'll have to make a complete report to General Merritt, of course."

46

"Try to move it along, please. I don't believe Captain Ritchie is anticipating my company with any great pleasure."

"Pleasure has nothing to do with it," Ritchie snapped. "I simply called attention to your apparent carelessness about military routine."

Starke's grin was a little crooked as he said quietly, "An error on my part, sir. Carelessness is a major sin in my language."

Colonel Haney intervened hastily, clearly annoyed that the two younger men should be rubbing each other the wrong way. "Take him along to your camp, Captain. Outfit him completely but keep the whole matter as quiet as possible. Please remember that this camp is quite easy to enter and that someone was mighty anxious to kill Lieutenant Starke this evening. They might even try again — if they can locate him."

It was not a pleasant thought for Starke to carry away with him. Nor could he feel very happy about the attitude of Captain Ritchie. Starke decided that he was going to have a problem with the stocky officer. If he had to depend on Ritchie for the sort of cooperation which seemed to be a part of the immediate future, he would have to do something about improving relations. It wasn't good policy for a man to have an enemy for a backer.

They proceeded in silence to another section of the sprawling camp, crossing an open stretch between camp areas and entering a section that was under a more alert guard. They were challenged briskly as they approached and Starke could see the bulky shapes of freight wagons in the gloom. It wasn't hard for him to guess that this would be the material intended for secret shipment to Juarez.

Ritchie did not explain, however. He simply pointed to a sizable tent and said briefly, "Your quarters, mister. Sergeant McCall will bring you a uniform in the morning."

Starke let it go at that. For the moment he was glad enough to relax within a guarded camp. Not since leaving the hill country of Coahuila had he known such a luxury. Tonight he would sleep; tomorrow he would seek the answer to some of the puzzles.

It was full daylight when he awakened at the touch of a hand on his shoulder. It was a long bony hand with freckles and a light thatch of red hair on it. At the other end of a blue-clad arm was a face to match. The man seemed to be hunched over as though about to play leapfrog, and Starke almost came up fighting. Then he saw that it was simply the case of an immensely tall man having to bend over awkwardly in the cramped quarters.

"Sergeant McCall reporting, sir," the tall man said, throwing a salute that was something of a masterpiece when the circumstances were taken into account. The sergeant looked awkward from one end of his gangling length to the other. Even under the best conditions his salute should have been clumsy. It wasn't. Even in the tent he managed it well.

Starke sat up. "Glad to know you, Sergeant. What is the good word this morning?"

McCall grinned at the tone, relaxing perceptibly. A smart noncom didn't need any more of a hint than that. "Same routine, sir. I brought a full uniform. Captain Ritchie's orders." Then he added doubtfully, "You'd better try it on, sir. I kind of imagine we'll need to make some swaps."

Starke reached out to pick up the bundle which had been placed on a packing box. "You know about me, Sergeant?"

"Yes, sir. We've been hearing a lot of tales about you since we arrived here in Texas."

"Most of 'em lies," Starke laughed. "I mean have you had any orders about me today — or last night."

"Yes, sir. You're second in command of our special section."

"Special section for what?"

"Handlin' them wagons out there, sir. I thought you'd know."

Starke held up a pair of cavalry breeches that would have fitted a man twice his girth. "I'm afraid Captain Ritchie doesn't approve of me," he said slowly. "Not only does he neglect to mention certain rather important details, but he doesn't seem to think I should wear clothes that fit me."

"Sorry, sir. I got the . . ."

"I understand. Can you trade these in for others?"

"Trust me, sir. In this camp a man can do right well if he knows how to handle things." He started out but turned to add in a low tone, "Don't let the captain rile you, sir. He's a good officer for all he's a mite thin-skinned on some matters."

49

That left Starke with another point or two for consideration. He decided that it would be interesting to learn more about his sulky captain and the quiet-spoken sergeant. For one thing, it would be good to know what was meant by that last remark of Sergeant McCall.

Within the next half hour he had a chance to pick up a bit of that information. McCall returned quickly with a presentable uniform which fitted well enough and Starke went out to look at the camp around him. By daylight he saw that it was really a wagon park where twenty wagons had been spanned out in a rectangle. A sentry stood at each corner of the quadrangle, and every wagon's canvas was tightly closed. The tents of the guard platoon had been pitched within the enclosure and no other outfit was quartered within two hundred yards.

There was a show of formality around the cooking fires when Starke emerged, but he quickly put the men at ease, accepting reasonably cooked rations from a squatty man who seemed to be cook for the outfit. Sergeant McCall had already eaten, but at Starke's request he remained by the fire to answer questions.

"I may not be with you very long," Starke told him, "but while I'm here I don't want to be ignorant. What outfit is this? Or what was it before it became a guard detail?"

"Headquarters Company." McCall grinned. "Colonel Haney asked for a detail that would stay with these wagons permanent. Captain Ritchie and the first platoon of the headquarters company drew the chore.

50

We've been nurse-maidin' these buggies for about three months now."

"Why a headquarters company?" Starke asked curiously.

"Choice was up to Major Mallory of Supply, sir. He picked Captain Ritchie."

Starke looked up with a crooked smile. "Go on. There's more to the yarn than that. Why Ritchie?"

The sergeant's lean length seemed to hunch up a little. "I ain't one to gossip about a commandin' officer, sir, but I reckon you got a right to know. Cap'n Ritchie's some sweet on Major Mallory's daughter. She's with the army and I suppose it seemed like a real good way to keep in touch with Supply. The major kinda likes Cap'n Ritchie, I reckon."

Starke didn't care too much for that information. A man ought to be carefully selected for this job; instead there had been some personal wire-pulling done. No wonder Colonel Haney had been a bit reserved in his treatment of Ritchie.

"A while ago you said Captain Ritchie was thin-skinned. Now it seems like he's also a good politician."

"Don't get me wrong, sir," McCall pleaded. "Ritchie and me were buck privates together in the Army of the Potomac. He got a battlefield commission durin' the first day at Gettysburg when we were delayin' the Rebs to let our army come up. He earned it. He's a good officer, but he gets a bit stiff when he runs across a West Pointer. I figure he expects the other feller to look down on him."

"You're quite a philosopher, Sergeant," Starke said seriously. "I'll respect your confidence. Thanks. Now tell me more about the stuff you've got in these wagons."

"Captain's got the manifests, sir, but I can tell you what's on 'em. Two hundred and fifty Enfield muskets with bayonets. Forty thousand rounds of musket ammunition — cartridges. Two hundred-odd uniforms, discarded in the first year of the war by some New York Zouaves who suddenly decided that parade pants weren't meant for the Virginia swamps. Six cases of dragoon pistols and another ten cases of assorted pistols captured from the Rebs. Ammunition in odd lots to fit all of 'em. No rations."

"Food's no problem," Starke told him. "The shipment is just what they'll need to do some recruiting. When the peons learn that Juarez can outfit 'em in red pants, they'll flock to join up."

"You figure you can get 'em through, sir?"

"I'm figuring to try."

"Do we help you?"

"That remains to be seen. So far I've learned more from you than from anybody else. Maybe by tonight I'll see what headquarters has in mind."

CHAPTER
FIVE

Captain Ritchie did not put in an appearance until the morning was half gone, but Starke did not let the time go to waste. The redheaded sergeant was clearly impressed with the reputation of "Serranias" Starke and flattered to be accepted in such a cordial fashion by him. In exchange for this cordiality Sergeant McCall expressed himself with considerable freedom, offering the considered opinions of a smart veteran who had learned to estimate his officers and his enemies.

Starke knew better than to place much dependence upon gossip, but it became fairly certain that he was due to deal with a couple of odd characters. Captain Ritchie was a gallant young officer who had been promoted a trifle too rapidly for his own balance. After winning his bars the hard way, he had come to be a stickler for formalities.

Major Mallory, chief of the Supply section, was the other officer to be considered. The wagon train was still officially under his command, and it appeared that he was no military man at all but a good provisioner who had been handed a wartime commission. Sergeant McCall made no attempt to hide his scorn of Mallory's methods.

Captain Ritchie came in brusquely shortly after ten. "Orders to report to Colonel Haney for a conference, mister," he snapped. "We'll stop to introduce you to Major Mallory on the way over. That's orders also." He didn't seem to like the latter idea for some reason.

Ten minutes later the two of them rode across a brushy ridge into another part of the camp, which had been out of sight from the smaller wagon park. Freight wagons and piles of supplies stretched out for half a mile. Everywhere men bustled about, troop details drawing supplies for their various units, while wagoners unloaded additional materials into the already large stacks of crates, boxes, and barrels. Starke concluded that this army had come well supplied.

Ritchie led the way to a large tent where two men talked soberly. One of the pair wore the blue trousers and boots of an officer but carried no insignia on his fresh white shirt. The other man was immaculate in a suit of gray civilian clothing.

The newcomers dismounted a little to one side of the tent opening, and Starke found time to estimate the man he realized was Major Mallory. At first glance it appeared that McCall had been correct: Mallory didn't look like a soldier but somehow suggested a successful accountant. He was a little pudgy, somehow mildly pompous, and nervously vague in his constant gesturing.

It was not Mallory who took first note of the visitors. Instead the civilian swung to face Starke, a pair of penetrating dark eyes studying the tanned face openly. The man was a shade under six feet, slender but with a show of strength beneath the gray frock coat. He was clean-shaven except for a bushy but well trimmed mustache, and he smiled as though well pleased at what he now saw.

"Lieutenant Starke, I believe," he said quietly. "I didn't expect to meet you so soon, although I understood that you had arrived in camp."

Both Mallory and Ritchie looked around in surprise. Mallory recovered himself to ask, "Did you say Starke? You know him?"

The civilian laughed. "Not personally. We've never met, but I've heard lots about him. He'll know me in the same manner, I imagine. My name is Rose, Robert Rose."

Starke concealed his astonishment. Rose's twisted smile indicated that he was enjoying his own bold play and Starke saw no reason to add to the enemy's pleasure. "I've heard of you," he said shortly. "A mite out of your territory in a Federal camp, aren't you?"

"Like yourself. Times change our ways, you know."

"Meaning that you've switched sides?"

Rose's smile faded a little, but he kept his calm tone. "Only one side left to take now. I can't sell supplies to a Confederate army any longer, so I sell them to the only army I can find."

Starke ignored the hint of challenge in the final statement. He was trying to guess why a man like Rose was playing his game so boldly. "You're lucky to find your ex-enemies so forgiving," he said, his tone expressionless.

"You're being a little insulting, mister!" Major Mallory exclaimed. "Mr. Rose is a contractor in whom I have complete confidence."

Starke nodded. "So it would appear. You will pardon me, sir, if I fail to share your confidence."

Mallory started another protest, but Rose interrupted. "No harsh words, gentlemen. As old enemies Lieutenant Starke and I understand each other quite well. Let us leave it that way." He turned pointedly to Major Mallory and went on as though dismissing the others, "Then we will make a beef delivery on the day after tomorrow? Is that satisfactory?"

Mallory was still showing signs of annoyance, but he managed to express his agreement. "Five hundred head — and they must be prime."

"None but the best," Rose said with a chuckle. "And now I'll leave before your Lieutenant Starke wants to start a war all over again."

The cool nerve of the man left Starke at a loss for words. There seemed to be no doubt about Rose's being leader of the secret guerrilla force which had been organized along the border. Yet Rose had the run of an important Federal camp, apparently handling a beef contract of continuing importance. No wonder the guerrillas were so well informed on matters relating to army plans.

Captain Ritchie broke the silence. "It would seem that your uniform won't be much of a disguise, mister. If that's the man you were talking about last evening he'll soon pass the word."

56

"What's all this?" Major Mallory broke in testily. "You're talking all around me."

"Sorry, sir," Ritchie apologized. "Your friend Rose has been reported as a rather dangerous enemy, leader of a group who tried to intercept Lieutenant Starke last night. Starke's whereabouts will now be known to his enemies."

"Nonsense. Rose is a civilian and not interested in either politics or military matters."

Starke thought of his experiences of the past evening and wanted to give Mallory a quick answer. Then he realized that it wouldn't do a bit of good. Both Mallory and Ritchie were making it rather clear that they did not expect to pay too much attention to the opinions of a junior officer. "Very well, sir," Starke murmured. "Hadn't we better move on to meet Colonel Haney, Captain?"

Ritchie seemed only too glad to get away. "No time to waste," he agreed. "Sorry to rush off, Major, but we're due for a conference in a few minutes. I wanted you to know Starke in case you have occasion to deal with him on the matter of those wagons."

"I'll remember him," Major Mallory said crisply. Starke had a definite impression that the major's memory would not be a pleasant one. Which made it mutual.

Ritchie was somewhat less distant as they rode away from Supply headquarters. "You're sure this man Rose is the one you mentioned to Colonel Haney?" he asked.

"Not much doubt about it. His own words were acknowledgment."

"I suppose so. Do you think he's been getting information from Mallory?"

"Your guess is as good as mine. It sure looks that way."

"Then we'd better let Haney know."

Starke didn't comment. He was thinking that the most important part of it from his personal viewpoint was that this camp represented no particular refuge for Fred Starke while Robert Rose could enter it with his followers whenever it so pleased them.

"I'll suggest to Colonel Haney that we put an agent or two at the job of watching Rose when he's in camp," Ritchie murmured. "That should take care of things."

Starke nodded solemnly. "By all means. Rose will be disappointed if we don't."

Ritchie frowned. Then he seemed to make up his mind that the remark was intended as a sarcasm and he fell silent, the frown almost a grimace.

Neither one spoke again until they came out from behind a stack of ammunition boxes. Then Ritchie snapped out an exclamation of anger. "That rascal sure has got his nerve! He must have an idea that he owns this camp!"

Starke looked ahead and saw that Robert Rose was perhaps a hundred feet away, sitting his horse with complete aplomb and talking animatedly with a blonde girl on a white horse. There could be no mistaking the girl: she was the sunburned blonde of the previous afternoon.

"You sound disturbed," Starke said curiously.

Ritchie ignored him. "I don't care what the old man says; Sue has got to stay away from that renegade!"

Starke began to understand. "Is that Miss Mallory ahead?" he asked.

"Of course." Ritchie didn't even look around. "She's got no business talking to a man like Rose. I don't care what her father thinks."

The stocky man was urging his horse forward and Starke let him draw away, content to speculate on the scene before him. For a moment he hoped that Ritchie would start some sort of fuss which would result in an open conflict, but Rose was too sharp for that. He pretended to take his leave in a casual manner, waving a nonchalant hand at Ritchie as he turned to ride away. It was all done very neatly and the retreat didn't seem like one at all. Instead, it had the effect of leaving an angry officer staring at Miss Mallory when there seemed to be no possible reason for him to show such anger.

The blonde girl stared perplexedly. "What in the world is wrong with you, Ned?" she asked. "You look ready to bite."

"How much did you tell that bandit?" he growled.

Her frown of astonishment relaxed a little as she looked past him and saw Starke. "I understand," she said quickly. "Your manners have been contaminated. You're trying to talk like Lieutenant Starke."

That stopped Ritchie. "How do you . . . ? What do you mean about . . . ?"

"Miss Mallory and I have met before," Starke cut in. "Obviously Mr. Rose has been identifying me to her.

59

Now she's trying to show off her new information and at the same time insult both of us."

The girl laughed aloud. "You are entirely too smart, sir. I hoped to astonish you with my information."

"Did Rose ask you any questions?" Starke inquired.

"Come now," she countered. "I do not reveal the confidences of others."

"Don't play games, Sue," Ritchie warned. "That fellow Rose is dangerous. If he tried to pump any information out of you we want to know what it was."

For a moment it seemed that she would refuse to take him seriously, but Starke added an explanation. "It was Rose's men who tried to ambush me yesterday. Captain Ritchie is entirely right in his warning. Did the man ask you any questions?"

"Only about you. When he discovered that I didn't know you he said that I would soon meet the famous Lieutenant Starke and would discover that we had already met under somewhat odd circumstances. That was when he rode away."

"Proof enough that he had a hand in the ambush. Otherwise he wouldn't have known so much." He turned to the puzzled Ritchie and sketched in the story, playing down the danger a little where it applied to Miss Mallory. "You can see how it all fits," he concluded. "Rose knew that I must be in camp because I slugged one of his sentries on the way in. Also, he knew that I was the one who slipped through his outer picket line when Miss Mallory diverted the attention of his sentries."

The girl's smile was brightly humorous. "You didn't sound quite so charitable about it yesterday afternoon," she commented.

"My mistake. Yesterday I was concerned only with avoiding notice. I didn't realize that they were actually looking for me. Now I know I was lucky that you happened along when you did."

"Clever me." She laughed. "But don't mention it to my father. I haven't thought it wise to bother him with the matter."

"No fear. Your father and I didn't reach very confidential terms. Just stay in camp and don't risk anything with this man Rose and I'll try to keep your secret."

He broke off to stare at her thoughtfully. "Maybe you can do more than that," he added, his voice dropping a little. "Somebody ought to keep an eye on Rose — and your father insists on thinking him an honest man."

"That's enough of that!" Ritchie exclaimed. "I'll not have Miss Mallory assuming any such risks as you seem to have in mind. If Rose is as dangerous as you say, she must stay completely away from him."

"She must take no risks, of course," Starke agreed. "But Rose will be in and out of the camp often — unless I miss my guess. Miss Mallory can certainly keep her eyes open when he is around."

"I'll not have it!" Ritchie snapped.

Starke caught the girl's eye and winked. "That settles that," he said meekly. "Captain Ritchie is in command, of course. However, you ought to know that there is some sort of plot on foot to keep us from moving certain supplies across the border. Quite a large number of former Confederate troops are either in the pay of the Mexican Imperials or are setting themselves up as outlaw raiders with the idea of loot in mind. We have reason to believe that Robert Rose is one of their principal leaders."

"That will be quite enough of that, mister," Captain Ritchie said sternly. "I told you that I did not want Miss Mallory involved. I consider it a violation of my orders that you have gone ahead to explain such a situation to her!"

"Nonsense!" The girl laughed, trying to ease the tension. "Don't be so stuffy, Ned."

"Forward!" Ritchie ordered, his eyes angry as he stared straight at Starke.

Starke saluted just a little too formally. Then he bowed to Miss Mallory. "You will forget everything I have said, of course," he murmured, one eyelid dropping slightly.

She winked openly in return. "When our good captain commands, how can we do otherwise?"

Ritchie did not speak again until they reached Colonel Haney's tent. Even then it was Starke who pursued the unfinished bit of unpleasantness. As soon as they were seated in the undercover information officer's quarters he asked directly, "Will you please make my status clear, Colonel? Captain Ritchie has seen fit to issue orders concerning the matter at hand, orders which I consider to be opposed to my own best interests and safety. If I am not to have a free hand I certainly do not propose to assume responsibility."

Haney looked both surprised and annoyed. "In the matter of handling those wagons, mister, you have a free hand. I thought that was clear."

"Not quite, sir. Preparations for the movement can be just as important to me as the move itself. I want to know what dangers are ahead before I pull out of this camp."

"You won't take the wagons out," Haney told him. "That's Captain Ritchie's job. It will be up to you to take delivery and to make the border crossing."

"Even so, sir, it is important that I have a free hand in trying to find out what troubles are likely to come up."

"Has Captain Ritchie been your trouble?" Haney asked with a grin. "If so, he's being pretty foolish. If I were going out into the border country with a convoy, I'd want to get the best advice possible. At the moment you seem to have the best supply of that advice."

Suddenly Ritchie seemed to reach a conclusion. "Let's forget it, sir. I think Starke and I can get together all right. Suppose we get on to the matter at hand?"

"Not yet," Starke said suddenly, his voice dropping a little. "I'd like to have a better look at what's coming past the tent."

The other two men stared silently at the ramshackle wagon which a cadaverous mule was hauling slowly along the company street. A tarpaulin partly covered a few vegetables in the vehicle, while an enormous straw hat did the same for the somnolent driver. The slack reins hinted that the mule was entirely on his own.

"Watch him, Captain!" Starke growled. "Keep your gun handy."

CHAPTER
SIX

There was a moment or two of tense silence, then Ritchie's hand began to inch away from his gun butt. "Don't be dramatic, mister," he scoffed. "You can't get suspicious of every stranger just because you think somebody's gunning for you."

"I'm suspicious of this one," Starke retorted. "Even the laziest peon wouldn't trundle through an army camp in his sleep. That fellow's faking and I want to know why."

Ritchie's hand went back to his gun and his voice took on a note of excited belief as he exclaimed, "I see what you mean! When a man tries so hard to look harmless, he's probably all the more dangerous."

Colonel Haney laughed shortly. "Then appearances are certainly deceitful in this case. The man doesn't even look alive."

Starke knew that the man on the wagon could overhear the words and he was ready for some sort of move. When it came he was still surprised. The sleepy Mexican did not even raise his head — in fact, only his calm tones indicated that he was actually awake. In excellent English he said, "You distort a fine bit from Diogenes, sir. The correct quotation is, 'If appearances are deceitful, then they do not deserve any confidence when they assert what appears to be true.' In substance, however, you are correct. Perhaps I am not so clever with the disguise."

"Diego!" Starke exclaimed, surprise and mirth mingling in his tone. "What kind of game are you playing?"

"Stop me," the Mexican said, his voice just loud enough for the trio to hear it. "Pretend to be interested in my vegetables."

"A friend of mine," Starke said quickly. "Pretend to be interested in his stuff. It's better if I don't seem to be talking to him. Someone may be watching."

Ritchie took the cue neatly, striding out into the company street to halt the pretended peddler as though suspicious of his load. There was a brief altercation, in which Diego made many useless motions while Ritchie fired a series of harsh questions. Through it all Starke could see that Diego was getting his information across to Ritchie.

Under cover of the play-acting Colonel Haney asked, "Who is this man and what is he trying to do?"

"A Juarez lieutenant, sir. You can trust him implicitly, so try to get a good look at him in case you ever need to know him."

There was little time for further exchange of information. Already Captain Ritchie was waving the Mexican on, apparently a little disgusted at the whole affair. When he turned to join the other two, however, he was grinning with satisfaction.

"Smart man there," he commented. "Speaks English like an educated man and plays his part to the hilt."

"A Harvard graduate, I believe. He lived in New Orleans with Juarez for some years. Incidentally, my congratulations on your own dramatic ability. If Rose has any of his men watching, I think they'll find nothing suspicious here."

"I'm not sure I like this," Haney grumbled. "It rubs me the wrong way that we should have to use such methods right in our own camp."

"I hope some other folks get annoyed enough to do something about it," Starke retorted. "In this instance the important thing is to keep Diego from being spotted. He's skating on thinner ice than I am. What was it he had to tell, Captain?"

"Nothing important now," Ritchie growled. "Since we've met Rose, we already know most of it. Your friend claims that the reason you were to be caught yesterday was so that the enemy could substitute one of their men for you. That man would then move the Juarez wagons directly into the hands of the Mexican Imperials. There's no doubt but what our mysterious enemy knows about everything that happens in this camp."

"Obviously," Starke murmured. "Rose gets every bit of information he needs firsthand."

Ritchie explained that to Haney in blunt terms, mentioning Major Mallory by name. Starke was content to have it so. Ritchie might yet turn out to be a good ally.

They discussed the matter at some length, but then Haney dropped his air of nonchalance and issued sharp orders. "Captain Ritchie, you will return to your command and take due precautions. Double the guard on those wagons every night from now on. Warn your men that there may be some attempt to destroy the wagons. If you need more men let me know. However, I'd prefer to stick to the present force. Less tongues to wag.

"Lieutenant Starke! You will wait here until I return. I mean to have the ear of General Merritt without further delay. We must make plans."

Starke nodded. "You might suggest to him that he order a general troop movement, sir. That would conceal the handling of the wagons."

Haney stared and Starke added, "General maneuvers. Throw the enemy off guard."

Captain Ritchie grunted irritably. "Still telling us how to run this army, I see."

"Any objections?" Starke snapped back. There was little of the Texas drawl in his voice now, only the sharp mixture of intonations resulting from his years with German settlers and Spanish-speaking people on the other side of the border. Somehow the combination came to the fore when he was annoyed.

"Stop it, both of you!" Haney ordered. "I can't have you two fighting with each other."

He stalked out immediately and Ritchie followed him. Starke let his gaze follow them only to the tent flap, and then he went back to sprawl on a cot while he let his grim thoughts run. This reunion with the army wasn't turning out to be quite what he had anticipated.

For some minutes he thought about the peculiar mess that had developed in Texas, but then he remembered Susan Mallory and his worried frown changed to a rather rueful grin. Quite a gal, that Sue. Too bad she had to be tied up with Ritchie.

He forced himself to forget her, concentrating on the problem he had been handed. Twenty wagonloads of contraband had to be hauled some three hundred miles across a guarded border. The army would help only just so far. Beyond that strict limit he would be on his own. No one would move to help him if he got into trouble. He would be an outlaw to both sides.

By the time he had sweated out the heat of the afternoon he could find no idea better than the one he had suggested to Colonel Haney. It would mean full cooperation from head-quarters, as well as better relations with Captain Ritchie. The latter sounded unlikely.

Colonel Haney was hot and irritably inclined when he came in. "Had to keep you waiting," he greeted. "That's what happened to me. The General's so fired up over his party tonight that he wouldn't see me after all." He sat down, wiping his forehead. "Hot as hell, ain't it?"

"Always is this time of year," Starke told him. "It'll be worse below the border."

"Then I'm glad it's you and not me who is going down that way. Did you come up with a plan yet? I rather thought you might if I were to leave you alone for a while."

Starke gave him an answering grin. So far Colonel Haney was the bright spot in the picture. The man had ideas. "I would like to suggest, sir, that a general movement should take place, something that would look like maneuvers on a large scale. Regiments or battalions should move out in all directions, each convoying a baggage train large enough to supply them for a period of two weeks or more. Let the majority of the units move directly toward the Rio Grande. They will take the attention of our enemies so that the really important move will be only a part of the bigger movement. A fast shuffle of stations within the camp just prior to the march should serve to hide the identity of the Juarez wagons. On the march each unit will move under strong guard, not letting strangers come in close enough to examine their baggage train. If that is carried out well enough I think the enemy will have a bit of trouble in determining which outfit to trail. By the time they get the Juarez wagons spotted they should be pretty well scattered, since they will have to divide their forces to trail so many wagon trains at first."

"You actually believe that these Texans would venture to attack a force of United States cavalry? Surely they would realize that doing so would result in stern measures. We have strong forces along the Rio Grande and the Gulf. A raid such as that would certainly cause General Sheridan to order stern military measures — and the rebels would know it."

Starke let the suspicion of a shrug become his answer. Then he amplified it by saying briefly, "The Confederacy surrendered in April. Texans attacked

United States troops at Palmetto Ranche in May. They won the battle too."

"But this is practically October. Those die-hards have gotten out of the country."

"Maybe some of them came back. Anyway, they don't have to use direct methods. When I first planned to raid the supply trains coming from Tampico into Texas I had the same problem. My Mexican supporters knew that any thrust against Imperial troops — who were convoying the trains — would result in a strong campaign against the holdouts in the hills. We didn't want to bring down any strong forces on the heads of our comrades, so we used strategy."

"What kind?"

"We played Indian."

Haney looked a little bothered. "But didn't it . . . ?"

"It was no time to be squeamish. In order to make our first raids look like the work of Indians, we played it up to the hilt. No survivors were permitted to escape. A few prisoners were taken back into the hills, but mostly my men were not interested in taking captives, especially European mercenaries who had taken pay to hunt them down like wild animals. We killed, burned, and scalped. It was that kind of war."

"And you think these Texans would adopt the same sort of ruse?"

"I'd bet on it. General Sheridan might hesitate to declare full martial law in Texas if the evidence indicated that an army supply train had simply been looted by Comanches or Apaches." He stared gloomily

70

at the ground for a moment before adding, "I'd do it that way if I were in their boots."

"It's hard to believe that . . ." Haney began.

"Take my word for it," Starke said harshly. "I told you that this isn't a nice kind of war that's fought down here. I know. I've been through it. Many of these men who are against us now have been through the same campaigns. They've fought Indians and they know Indian methods. They hate Yankees in general — and they hate me in particular. Don't ever get to thinking that they'll fight it out on polite lines."

Again he paused briefly before making an addition: "Sorry if I sound grim, sir. And I don't mean to be sounding off to a superior officer. I simply know what I'm talking about, and it's my hide that's the main target right now."

"No offense taken," Haney said. "I believe you. We called you in because we wanted your advice. I'm planning to take it."

"About the large movement to conceal the handling of the wagons?"

"We'll have to take that one up with General Merritt tomorrow morning. But I'm with you all the way."

"Then we don't get anything started tonight?"

Haney shook his head. "As I said before, we're going social this evening. General Merritt has an idea that he would like to cement good relations with the local inhabitants. Some of that war-is-over-let's-be-friends sort of thing. At the same time we'll have a dedication of the permanent buildings that have been put up. This is to be a regular post, you know."

"I hope he locates friendlier local people than I've met," Starke said gloomily.

"I suggest that you make it a point to attend," Haney went on. "I'll be interested in knowing what kind of civilian guests show up. In fact, I think I'll make it an order. You are hereby detailed to attend the party and to keep your eyes open. Captain Ritchie will show you how to reach the spot. And go armed."

"What about dress? I have nothing in the way of dress uniform. Or did you mean that I appear with side arms and make noises like a provost?"

Haney smiled. "We'll all wear whatever we have. You're all right as you are. And carry your gun inside your shirt."

Starke saluted briskly and went out.

A brief September twilight was bringing a measure of relief to the heat-drenched country when Starke climbed the gentle rise of ground that they were calling Government Hill. He had been given his directions by Sergeant McCall, since Captain Ritchie had not shown up at the wagon camp. McCall hinted that Ritchie would be in town getting himself shaved especially close for his evening at the party with Miss Mallory. Starke had taken the information rather glumly, his annoyance increased by the realization that he had no reason to feel disturbed. Miss Mallory had been pleasant, but nothing more. There was no excuse for being jealous of Captain Ritchie.

Still, his mind kept coming back to the idea even as he climbed the gentle slope of Government Hill. Lanterns winked along its paths and a double row of

72

lights on the crest indicated the partly finished buildings which would be the nucleus of the permanent post. That sight and the knowledge that many of the arriving guests were former Confederates helped Starke to force his thoughts away from Susan Mallory. Tonight he would be surrounded by blood enemies. Tonight he couldn't afford to let his wits go wool-gathering.

He quickly found a spot from which he could observe the arrival of guests, most of the civilians coming on horseback, although a few couples arrived in carriages. Starke didn't attempt to enter the main hall until a burst of band music heralded the opening of festivities, and then he managed to slip into a knot of junior officers, who obviously were getting themselves ready to become a stag line. From that cover he hoped that he would be able to watch the civilians unobserved.

The opening of the formal program, which was to precede the dancing, was brief and punctual. General Merritt, looking rather undistinguished in a plain uniform, was introduced, and he proceeded to speak in a voice that suggested some uneasiness. Starke prepared himself to endure a dreary speech but suddenly found that he was listening intently. Merritt was not an orator, but tonight he was saying something that made his words worth hearing.

There had been something of a rustle among the guests at the start, but Merritt quickly caught his audience, dropping his air of hesitancy as he launched into the main part of his speech. Speaking first of the need for an army post at this particular point, he went quickly to the desire for a good post name. Fort Sam Houston, the post was to be called, he told them. The United States could be proud in naming a fort for a loyal Texan who had at the same time been a loyal American.

There was more of it, but not too much, a clever prodding of former Secessionists in the audience and an appeal to those who were now willing to admit error. He ended with a plea for a united country and referred bluntly to the danger of imperialism in Mexico. Starke wondered whether the State Department would approve of the open reference and decided that this was strictly army. Probably General Sheridan had been behind the remark, meaning it to be a warning both to Maximilian and to the former Rebels who were proposing to join the Imperialists.

On that sober note the opening of the party ended. Some people moved out at once as directions were given for reaching the various dances being held by individual units. Starke decided to remain at the headquarters party. The big game ought to show up here.

Almost at once he got something of a shock. Diego Menendez and the girl called Lirio were in the room, both of them garbed flawlessly in well cut American clothing. Both seemed completely at ease and prepared to enjoy themselves.

He caught Diego's eye but drew a blank stare that brought him sharply to his senses. He must not show any recognition of either of them. No enemy must

74

connect him with either — yet it seemed likely that they had come to deliver some sort of message.

While he was considering the problem he saw Captain Ritchie come into the hall with Susan Mallory. The blonde girl was laughing gaily, as strikingly pretty in an evening gown as she had been in riding costume. Starke noted that the healthy tan of her face and neck shaded off smoothly into the lighter color of her bare shoulders. Evidently she must take some pains to avoid the sharp contrast between the two areas, probably to the extent of taking regular sun baths.

The thought intrigued him, but at the same time he knew something akin to jealousy. Both Diego and Ritchie had fared very well with their partners of the evening. Lirio and Susan were easily the prettiest women in the hall.

He forced the thought from his mind, concentrating on the grimmer business at hand. Even now it was practically certain that some enemy had spotted him and would be observing his every move. He could not risk even a casual remark to Diego. There had to be some other way.

The dancing began promptly, the lively strains from a small regimental band giving the social function a rather military aspect. As the sets were formed Starke found a better opportunity to observe those present, quickly spotting Robert Rose. The guerrilla leader was escorting a yellow-haired girl who looked young enough to be his daughter but who was rather obviously seeking to destroy that illusion. Twice Starke saw Rose frown at her as she became a little too effusive. The sight told him that Rose, also, was not anxious to become too conspicuous.

A half hour of careful observation told him that Rose had at least three friends in the gathering, men who had taken covert signals from him on several occasions. Somewhat belatedly Starke realized that one of the trio was the fellow with the sideburns who had challenged him at Manuel's place. That suggested a disturbing thought. Maybe the men had stumbled on something that would connect Manuel's cantina with Starke.

Still, there was no indication that any of Rose's crowd were paying the least attention to Diego and Lirio. Like other men, they didn't hesitate to look at a girl who was pretty enough to be worthy of a second glance, but Starke could not see any indication that their attention to her was anything more than the casual interest of the male in the attractive female.

When he felt certain of that conclusion, he also knew something else about Diego and the girl. They were quite alone at the dance. Not once had either of them spoken to anyone else except as they danced. They were playing the role of polite guests, self-effacing but not unsociable.

At that point he decided that he would have to make a play. A dance had just ended, so he crossed the room to where Ritchie was trying to ward off the advances of a quartet of rivals. Starke pushed in without ceremony, his broad grin disarming as he took Susan's hand. "This one was to be mine, I believe," he announced. "Seems like I'd better file my claim before all of these ambitious lads make you forget me."

There was a brief hesitation on the part of the girl and a fleeting frown from Ritchie. Then they met Starke's direct glance and played up to his lead with some cleverness. "How could I forget?" Susan reproached him. "Captain Ritchie has been complaining all evening about having to look forward to this moment."

They bantered in that vein for a minute or two, eventually losing the young officers who had been unlucky enough to get in the way of necessity. By that time the music was starting again and Starke had to pass his message quickly, anxious not to make the meeting appear anything more than a matter of claiming a dance partner.

"Diego's here," he said. "That's him with the pretty Mex girl. See if you can dream up a way of meeting him without making anyone suspicious. It could be important."

Then he was moving out to the floor with Miss Mallory, wondering what he was going to do next. Three years of hard riding on the border hadn't put him in very good practice for a session of social dancing.

Susan Mallory seemed to understand a part of the strategy, at least. "Do we go on and dance," she asked quietly, "or shall we visit the punch bowl instead? If you're keeping an eye on something it might be well for you to remain along the sidelines."

"Especially since I'm badly out of practice with my dancing," he added with a wry smile. "Thanks for being most understanding. Lead the way to the punch and keep pretending that we have no thought in the world except for light social ideas."

"I should be able to do that well," she murmured. "Judging by your comments of yesterday afternoon you would expect me to play the thoughtless part with no effort at all."

He made a little bow, offering his arm. "My apologies once more. It becomes more and more apparent that I misjudged you."

She slipped her hand into the crook of his elbow. "Then we'll give you an opportunity to rearrange your judgments. I'm quite vain, you see."

"And suitably spoiled, of course. Somehow it becomes you."

CHAPTER
SEVEN

It was easy to play the role of infatuated swain, Starke found. Susan Mallory chatted gaily as they strolled through the edge of the crowd, keeping her remarks just pointed enough so that he could follow her references but vague enough so that anyone overhearing would have caught no bit of real information. Only when they were safe from prying ears did she ask quickly, "Who is the person you mentioned to Ritch?"

"Dark young man with the pretty Spanish-looking girl in white. They are not dancing just now. Don't look immediately, but you'll see them a little to the left of where General Merritt is sitting."

Her smile did not alter, but she began an idle scanning of the crowd, as though mildly interested in the gathering as a whole. "A friend of yours?" she pursued.

"Very much so. Since you've become one of our allies, you'd better make certain that you'll recognize him in case of need. He's a Mexican, but he was educated in the United States. He's loyal to Juarez and works hard for us because we are trying to help Juarez."

"You mean he likes us because he wants to use us?"

"Something like that. I depended upon his followers because I had to use them in my work against the Confederate supply lines. He feels much the same way about our people. But don't rate him too lightly on that account. I'd trust my life to him any day, just as he is trusting his to my discretion at this moment. He would be a marked man in Texas if I were to show any interest in him. That's why I asked Ritchie to try his hand at making some sort of contact."

She looked at him rather oddly. "I'm a little surprised that you depended upon Ned. Today you two didn't seem to hit it so well."

"That was all personal," he assured her solemnly. "Today he was annoyed that I should speak so familiarly to you. I was annoyed that he had the inside track with such a pretty girl. Tonight we both forget our differences because we must work together at something."

"You puzzle me," she complained. "Part of what you say always sounds so ridiculous, but the other part always seems to make sense. I don't know what to believe."

"By all means believe the part about the enemies we have with us. Try to remember the people I point out to you this evening. It's a deadly game and we need to be as well informed as possible."

She nodded quietly. "I think others must feel the same. Somehow I detect a sort of tension in the room all the time."

"Naturally. Our people are trying for the good will of the former enemy. Some of the former enemy are just as anxious to avoid more trouble. But most of them know that the others are planning to make trouble. It's those others we must guard against."

"Which ones?" she asked shortly.

He pointed out some of the men he had spotted, mentioning names where they were known but never looking directly at the people he was spotting for her. Miss Mallory played her role with fine skill, putting on a show of being gaily careless about everything.

Suddenly Starke chuckled. "This gets pretty funny, doesn't it? Yesterday I called you stupid. Tonight I'm handing you a responsibility I consider too deep for some senior officers. It doesn't quite make sense."

"I'm not sure I like the way you say that," she countered, keeping her smile. "I'll certainly try to keep my part of it from becoming ridiculous."

"I didn't mean it that way. I . . ."

"Don't protest too much. I'm flattered. Particularly when I think of how much your attitude has changed since yesterday. But don't you think we'd better make some sort of diversion for Ritchie? He's hesitating about closing in on your friend."

"Good reason," Starke muttered. "Half of the men in this room are looking at you and the other half are staring at Lirio. Diego should have come here with a partner who isn't quite so conspicuous."

"Look," she said suddenly. "There's one of the men who tried to kidnap me yesterday."

Her nod showed him the proper direction, and he saw that a bearded man in somewhat baggy broadcloth had come in and was standing close beside Robert

Rose. It was undoubtedly the fellow who had been called Eli. He was clean now and apparently sober, but he was still identifiable, particularly with the black eye he was sporting.

"That's our answer," he said. "If you're game to play up to it we'll go speak to Eli. Very polite and forgiving, of course, but Rose's gang will be watching us all the way. That'll take the attention away from Diego and his lady. If Ritchie takes the hint he'll have time to pass a few words with Diego."

"Won't this be dangerous for you?" she whispered, taking his arm as he started straight toward the men in question.

"Tonight we're all on good behavior," he replied. "Rose and his men are playing the bold hand. We'll do the same and see how they like it."

"Maybe we should accuse the fellow and have him arrested," she whispered. "That would stir up enough of a fuss so that Ritchie could hold a whole conference with your Diego."

"Don't hold grudges." He laughed. "Maybe we owe Eli a debt of gratitude. His blunder of yesterday has helped us. Anyway, it gave me a chance to meet you."

"What a beautiful meeting," she commented, almost giggling.

"Keep thinking like that and we'll try to puzzle them a bit."

They could see the uneasy shifting of feet as they approached the little group of civilians. Rose said something over his shoulder and Eli tried to get out of sight behind a man Starke had not previously noted.

The sudden silence in that part of the room was almost startling.

Miss Mallory played her part promptly and well. Offering her best smile, she extended a hand to Rose and spoke pleasantly. "So glad you could come, Mr. Rose. It's nice to feel that business friends can be social friends as well. You know Lieutenant Starke, I believe?"

Rose recovered his poise swiftly. "You are most kind, Miss Mallory. Thank you. Lieutenant Starke and I are old friends, of course."

"Fellow Texans from away back," Starke agreed, blandly cordial. "And I see another old friend back there. Come on out where we can see you, Eli. Don't be bashful at a happy time like this."

This time Rose faltered, and again there was a restless shifting of feet. Out of the corner of his eye Starke could see a pair of uniformed officers moving toward the spot, while behind them Colonel Haney was standing erect and watchful. Evidently the officer was puzzled by Starke's move and was sending tentative reinforcements.

Miss Mallory took over again. "Oh, yes," she exclaimed. "Our old friend Eli. We didn't expect to see you so soon again, especially here in camp. But whatever must have happened to you? Did you run into something?"

Eli grumbled something inaudible and shrank farther back toward the door. Three other men pushed in, vaguely threatening in their manner but still restraining themselves with some care. By that time everyone in the hall seemed to realize that something out of the ordinary was happening. The talk had ceased and even the bandsmen were watching.

Rose changed his manner abruptly. "What's your game, Starke?" he demanded.

"I could ask you the same question, but I won't. I already know."

"That's not the point. I mean this business now. Why are you trying to be funny about Eli?"

"Don't we deserve something for our troubles of yesterday?" Starke asked innocently. "Wouldn't you rather have us forgive and be friendly, instead of preferring charges against him? After all, he did make a violent attack upon Miss Mallory."

"Then go ahead and have him arrested." Somehow the words hinted that Rose would not have cared too much.

Starke smiled. "I suppose it would serve him right for blundering. But, really, we don't hold grudges. After all, his drunken foolishness gave me a chance to meet a very pretty young lady. I'd be ungrateful if I tried to punish him further."

"And I still have his gun," Miss Mallory said brightly. "It will make a wonderful souvenir."

Somebody laughed and Starke glanced around humorously at the circle of grim faces. "Don't take it so hard, gents," he advised. "When you team up with polecats like Eli you've got to expect fool plays. It's all right if you like to depend on comedians, but . . ." He shrugged and turned back to Rose, satisfied that he had taken a reasonably good inventory of the guerrilla chief's principal supporters. So far, the act was going very well. The only flaw was that the man with the sideburns was watching with very suspicious eyes.

With that in mind Starke continued, "But don't be too hard on Eli. As I said, he did me a good turn. Instead of sneaking into camp like the bedraggled peon I was trying to be, I was able to come in peaceful-like with Miss Mallory." He didn't know whether they would know that for a lie or not. It was worth mentioning on the off-chance that it would further confuse them.

Rose studied him narrowly. "Just what are you trying to gain by all this palaver, Starke?" he demanded. "You didn't come over here just to gloat over that fool Eli."

"Mr. Rose," Susan Mallory protested, "you do persist in discounting our hospitality. I think we'd better leave. No one seems to care for our presence at all."

"Southern gallantry has reached a low ebb," Starke agreed as he turned and offered his arm. "As a Texan I am humiliated."

She suppressed a delighted giggle as they moved back across the big room. Starke winked solemnly at the two officers who had moved in on his flank and the pair of them turned silently away. As if on cue, the band struck up a lively air and the tension melted away. Captain Ritchie was already back with a knot of fellow officers, while neither Diego nor Lirio were anywhere to be seen.

"I think it worked," Miss Mallory said as soon as she could control her mirth. "I certainly did enjoy seeing them all so flustered."

"Good fun," Starke agreed. "They were prepared to bluster out a defiance and were a bit at a loss when we elected to play it sweet. I'll bet they do some talking after they leave here, trying to figure out what it meant."

They went straight to Ritchie and Starke surrendered his partner with a low bow. Ritchie managed to look rather stern, but what appeared to be a conventional remark was really, "He passed me a note. I'll look at it later; they'll be watching you."

Starke replied, "Pass it to Colonel Haney. I won't speak to you again while they're here." Then he moved on, taking his place once more among the unattached junior officers. This was a funny way to fight a war, he thought. A man could get mighty confused.

Within the next twenty minutes he was interested to note that Rose and his crowd disappeared. They didn't go together and most of them made some show of speaking to various officers before departing, but it was clear that the signal had gone out for a withdrawal. Probably someone had remained behind as a scout, but Starke could not see anyone that he knew.

Eventually he drifted across to Colonel Haney, waiting until that officer had been entirely alone for some minutes. Haney motioned to a seat and asked, "What were you trying to do a while ago? For a minute or two we were afraid of trouble, especially when you had Miss Mallory with you."

Starke explained. "I hope it worked," he added. "I wouldn't want to be the means of putting that crowd onto Diego. His friends would be the first to suffer."

"I think your ruse worked. Ritchie played it safe, not even speaking to your friend as the message was passed to him. At the moment all eyes were turned toward the little drama you and Miss Mallory were playing."

"Not drama," Starke told him with a chuckle. "Farce comedy."

"There's not much comedy in the minds of the men you faced," Haney said shortly. "Look at this."

He handed over a thin strip of paper which evidently had been folded into very small compass. The writing too was small but also very neat. It read: *Floral boys definitely on Max payroll. First objective is your death. They have men in your camp. Be careful. D.*

Haney eyed him as he read it. "Your friend even makes jokes in English, I note."

"And he risked plenty to bring that message tonight. I suppose it means that he suspects some sort of plan to get me in a hurry."

"I read it that way also. Ritchie and I have made plans. Two men will accompany you when you leave here tonight. They will be armed and will have orders to shoot if anyone acts suspicious. For purposes of clouding the situation a trifle, they'll pretend to be provost guards escorting a prisoner. I trust you won't mind the indignity."

"As a matter of fact, I'm rather resentful of the whole situation. I find it hard to believe that Rose and his men feel safe in playing their tricks within the confines of an army camp. I'm afraid we'll not make much headway in controlling Texas while we let them think they can do as they please."

"Patience," Haney said. "We need time to identify our enemies. Pacifying the country and controlling guerrillas don't go well together, but we're trying to do both — and without interrupting the program of helping Juarez. I'd favor declaring our entire encampment as out-of-bounds for civilians, but politically it would seem unwise. For the present we will try to protect you."

"How long do you expect that to last?"

"Another twenty-four hours, I estimate. By that time you'll be on your way, protecting yourself as best you can."

"Good. I'll feel safer on my own than with five thousand men around me — five thousand who don't know who the enemy is."

They discussed the matter at some length, Starke trying to identify the men he had spotted as Rose's allies. Evidently Haney had not been idle during the dramatic sequence, for he was able to name seven of them. "Your move was a good one for me," he told Starke. "My agents have been gathering information and names, but you jolted them into rallying around Rose. Then I could verify my suspicions. We'll watch those gentlemen very carefully."

"Then you have men in the town?"

"Of course."

"Good. I'll remember that."

A lanky, redheaded sergeant came into the hall at that point and Starke smiled appreciatively. Sergeant McCall on the guard detail suited him perfectly. He smiled again as he watched McCall hesitate, as if the latter was dubious about entering a social affair of high-ranking officers. Then the tall sergeant stiffened and came toward Haney and Starke, his stiff bearing almost ludicrous.

The man halted two paces from them, saluting with snap and precision. "You sent for me, sir?" he asked.

Haney nodded. "I asked Captain Ritchie to detail two men who could be trusted implicitly. Who is the other one?"

"Private Maguire, sir. Acting corporal on the guard detail."

"Very good. From this moment you are to remain with Lieutenant Starke at all times. In public it will be well to let it appear that he is under some form of arrest. Actually you are to be alert against an attack upon him. There is a strong suspicion that some former rebels are in this camp with the intention of murdering him. Are you armed?"

"Yes, sir. Maguire is outside with the guns. Revolvers for both of us. I took the liberty of bringing one for the lieutenant also, sir."

"Good man. I think Mr. Starke is already armed, but it was a good idea. Just remember that you are not to take any orders from the lieutenant if such orders conflict with the orders I've just given you." Haney chuckled dryly as he added, "I imagine he'll object to what he may call nursing, but that is no reason why we will permit him to take risks. Do you understand?"

"Yes, sir."

"You're on duty until relieved. Captain Ritchie will issue the orders then."

Starke caught the half puzzled, half humorous glance from the lanky trooper and smiled easily. "I'll behave, Sergeant," he promised. "And it won't be long that you'll have to play wet nurse for me. I'll be getting away from here in a short time."

McCall winked, but his voice was without any shade of feeling as he said, "Very good, sir."

CHAPTER
EIGHT

The crowd had thinned out perceptibly by that time, but Starke was in no hurry to leave. He led the way to a corner where there was a bit of privacy and outlined the situation to Sergeant McCall. "I don't want to sound like an old woman," he concluded, "but a lot of the enemy were here tonight. It's just possible that they left someone to do what they want under cover of the excitement. We'll have to be ready."

"I understand, sir."

"Then pass the word to Maguire and stand ready at the door. I'll stick around here for a few minutes to see if I can spot anything off-color. We'll move in ten minutes."

There was still a bit of movement around the hall when the three of them set off down the gentle slope. The traffic was a measure of protection, but Starke did not let the fact put him off guard.

"We'll spread out a bit when we hit the hollow," he murmured to his companions. "It's the most likely spot for an ambush. Mac had better stay close behind me to protect the rear, while Maguire can flank out a dozen paces and stay abreast of me. We'll move as quietly as possible."

He saw that the two men followed orders smartly and with some skill. Evidently they were not going to follow too closely the part about not taking orders from him. It made him feel a little better about the whole affair. Both men seemed to be good sturdy characters and he was glad to have them on his side.

They moved into the questionable area, a brushy section which separated the construction area from the nearest troop camp. Starke was handling himself like an Apache now, his steps soft and as silent as he could make them. Neither of his companions were succeeding too well at the business of moving silently, but he didn't mind. If an enemy was in ambush ahead it might be just as well to let him feel that he was unsuspected. The important thing was to locate him quickly.

They were halfway across the brush area when it happened. A voice came sharply but in a hoarse whisper. "Starke? Is that you?"

Eyes accustomed to night scouting spotted the man at once. He was crouched behind a bit of mesquite just ahead and a little to the right, almost directly in front of Maguire. Starke went to the ground without a word, waiting until he saw Maguire do the same. A grunt from the rear indicated that McCall had also taken the hint. Then he called, "Who wants Starke? Say it quick; I've got you lined in my sights!"

The shadow moved swiftly to Stark's immediate front, a curse suggesting that the ambusher was baffled by his intended victim's movement. "Got to talk to yuh, Starke," he growled. "Stand up there and stop playin' the fool!"

"Your name!" Starke snapped again. "Fast or I shoot!"

The man came a step closer, searching in the darkness for the sound of the voice. "Don't talk loco, Starke," he replied. "Yuh ain't healed and I know it."

A sudden crackle of brush from Starke's right came at that moment. Instantly the stranger fired at the sound. A split second later Starke's gun blasted at the flash, two quick shots hammering hard on the heels of the first one. Then the night was darkly silent for a space of perhaps ten seconds.

It was Private Maguire who broke the tension. "Damn that brush!" he complained. "It sure can stick in a man's ribs."

"Are you hurt?" Starke asked.

"Nope. But the polecat sure took a swipe at me when I tried to git off'n that stuff that was stickin' me. Is he dead?"

"He ain't movin' none." It was McCall who replied.

Starke clambered to his feet then, his lips twisted into a mirthless smile in the darkness. "You boys get real useful," he declared in a low voice. "I was real curious to see if this jigger was alone. Now I know he was. Your gabbin' would have had bullets flying all around if there'd been anybody else along with him."

McCall chuckled. "Givin' us a lesson in brush fightin', mister?" he asked.

"You could call it that. In this country you don't take time out to celebrate your victory until you find out whether it might not be just the opening skirmish. Now let's have a look at our late friend before some nosey provost takes it into his head to come have a look."

McCall seemed to have taken a new lease on his confidence. "You know, Maguire," he said softly, "there's a certain lieutenant I could really git to like. He talks like a real nice feller. Now git on your feet and let's do what he says!"

"Any matches?" Starke asked, ignoring the comment.

McCall went forward, bending to strike a light above the fallen gunman. Starke looked closely, checking swiftly to make sure that the man was as dead as he appeared. "Eli," he said shortly. "No wonder he was nervous."

"You know him, sir?" Maguire asked.

"We've met. I talked to him tonight. He knew what he was supposed to do, of course, so he was a mite uneasy. Let's start moving; we'll let Colonel Haney decide what to do with the carcass."

He found Haney in his tent and reported the incident, suggesting that it might be a good idea to remove the body and keep the whole thing quiet in order to let the enemy do some guessing. Then he went back to the wagon camp with his new companions and turned in for the night.

When he awoke it was daylight and Captain Ritchie was already up and dressed. Starke had not heard the man come in, but the surly grunt of greeting suggested that the captain's lateness had not been occasioned by any happy circumstances. If Ritchie had remained with

94

Miss Mallory until a late hour he had certainly not come away in any festive humor.

Starke tried to soothe the man. "Thanks for your handling of that matter last night, Captain," he said easily. "It took a neat bit of doing not to give Diego away."

"Not the sort of doing you used," Ritchie snapped. "I can see no excuse for your ridiculous use of Miss Mallory. Placing her in a position of danger as you did was both foolhardy and inexcusable."

"Sorry. She seemed to enjoy it."

"That is not the point. Miss Mallory seems to enjoy a number of things which don't make too much sense. She needs protection. Instead, you force her into greater danger than her own inclination would suggest."

"My apologies. Please console yourself with the thought that I'll soon be on my way."

"And not a moment too soon!"

Starke left the tent without further comment. He thought he understood a part of Ritchie's sullenness and he didn't want to make it worse. Within a matter of hours he would be starting out on a dangerous mission, leaving behind him a man whose cooperation would be vital to his success. It didn't make sense to antagonize that man.

He ate his breakfast with McCall and Maguire, learning to his satisfaction that there was no talk in camp about the shooting. Someone had done a good job of getting rid of the dead man quietly.

While they were eating, an order was passed through the camps, a messenger relaying it orally to whatever officer seemed to be in charge of each unit. In the case of the wagon camp Starke was the individual addressed. "Orders from the General himself, sir," the courier said, saluting snappily. "All passes for civilians are canceled as of this moment. No one is to move from the camp of his particular unit until further orders and countersigns are arranged. Officers are to detain any persons now in their camps until such persons are released by orders from headquarters."

Starke acknowledged, nodding to McCall as the messenger rode away. "Better pass that on to Captain Ritchie," he said shortly. "I imagine I'll need to get on over to Colonel Haney's tent before they start to enforce the blockade."

He found Haney waiting for him a bit impatiently. "General Merritt is rushing matters a bit," the colonel grumbled. "I asked him to put a secrecy guard over the camp, but I didn't expect him to order it so soon. Where is Ritchie? And your guards?"

Starke grinned. "Ritchie's a bit unhappy about the way I used his lady friend as a smoke screen last night. I didn't ask him to come along. Sergeant McCall and Private Maguire seemed to think they were restricted by the new order."

Haney eyed him with shrewdness. "Which was just the chance you wanted to get away from them, I suppose?"

"Exactly, sir. I guess I've been on my own long enough so that so much spit and polish annoy me."

"We'll soon fix that, mister. The General wants to get you on the road immediately. That's why he clamped on this security restriction. Come along and we'll go talk to him."

There was no conversation between them as they walked across to headquarters, entering General Merritt's rather elaborate tent without more than a brief word to the orderly. Starke had already decided that Merritt was a smart officer in spite of his rather colorless appearance, and this morning he saw no reason to alter that estimate. The commander looked up sharply at the newcomers and snapped a quick greeting.

"Colonel Haney. Mister Starke. Good morning. Sit down and tell me what stage your planning has reached. You will notice that I've already taken steps to rid the camp of enemy spies."

"The plans are just as they were last evening, sir," Haney stated, taking a seat. "I suggest that Lieutenant Starke offer the program he has in mind."

"Very well. I'll be quite interested to hear from him." He turned a cordial smile at the younger man and added, "I've been hearing a lot about him ever since we started down here. Your work is well known, mister."

"Thank you, sir. I'm a little surprised to hear it. I understood that I was practically the forgotten man in military circles."

"I've told him about that," Haney interrupted. "Back pay and overdue promotion has already been taken up in official papers."

Merritt nodded again. "We'll try to take care of you, Starke. Now what do you propose as a plan for getting around these restrictions that are hampering us?"

"May I ask, sir, as to the extent to which the army will back me?"

"I thought that part had been made clear. General Sheridan has declared himself ready to offer open aid to Juarez. He has also stated that he considers Maximilian in the same class with the old buccaneer Morgan, a pirate to be rooted out by force if necessary. Our diplomatic service is not so bold. Washington commands us to avoid any violation of neutrality or of the Mexican border. Thus we cannot back you in any overt violation. Where we may do so without publicity we will help in any way to get that material to Juarez. Is that a sufficient statement?"

"I understand, sir. I am to do what the army would like to do but which they are ordered to refrain from doing."

"Correct. Now what do you have to tell me about the presence of guerrillas now reported to be in this vicinity?"

Starke told his story quickly, including each incident which had pointed up the presence of enemies in San Antonio and the camp itself. Merritt heard him through to the end before asking. "Do you believe those numbers you quoted? The ones about the number of men under arms south of the border?"

"Yes, sir. My source was the same one that told me that our army has fifty thousand men within striking distance; five thousand of them are here and another fifty-five hundred are under General Custer at Houston. At all posts they are in a state of readiness. About a quarter of the entire Texas command is cavalry, mostly veterans of the Shenandoah and Appomattox campaigns. Two regiments are armed with one of the new type repeating carbines, supposedly Spencers, while the others are carrying older weapons. Supplies are generally understood to be plentiful and of good quality."

Merritt glanced quizzically at Colonel Haney. "It would appear that someone along the border has organized an excellent spy service. Do you suppose it means we have traitors among us?"

"No, sir." It was Starke who answered, even though the query had been aimed mainly at Haney. "This command has moved into recently conquered country. You have enemies on every hand, no longer active enemies, of course, but men who would enjoy seeing something go wrong with this movement. They gather information and pass it along into Mexico, hoping that some harm may come from their efforts. Actually, I believe they're doing our cause some good. If this movement is calculated to impress the French and cause them to withdraw their support from Maximilian, it will be something of a help to let such facts go through."

"It's a point," General Merritt conceded. "But where did you get the information?"

"From Juarez agents. They're active too, you know. And hopeful."

"Very well. I'll tell you something else which you have permission to pass along discreetly. A shipment of thirty thousand muskets is now on its way from Baton Rouge. One way or another, we hope to get them across to Juarez without too much delay. But, meanwhile, what do you propose to do about the material we already have on hand?"

"Do I understand, sir, that it is my problem?"

"Of course. General Sheridan asked for you on that account."

Starke chuckled dryly. "Quite a surprise, sir. It was the first hint I'd had that anyone remembered my being down here."

"General Sheridan doesn't miss many tricks, young man. Just keep that in mind. Now get on with your story and tell me how you figure to move those wagons out of camp without getting the guerrillas on your tail."

"I'll not take them out, sir. The only chance is for me to arrange to meet them at a point where I can take over with my own men, relieving the army unit which has handled the wagons to that point."

"On this side of the border?"

"Of course, sir. I'll make the crossing. That is part of the whole arrangement. However, I'll be so completely on my own that I must have some measure of protection against the enemy. The only thing you can give me is secrecy."

"How do we go about getting it?"

"By a general troop movement, sir. This force is on maneuvers in country where some active demonstrations will not be amiss. Send out every available unit in a series of strong columns with baggage. One of those columns will be the outfit we're interested in, but watchers may have some trouble in deciding which one to follow. Perhaps the whole thing can be elaborated into a big training maneuver, but one way or another, every outfit involved must put on a show and keep watchers at a distance. Aim at least a dozen columns at the border and see to it that each unit guards its wagons carefully. Other columns can furnish further diversion by moving out into other directions. The real wagon outfit should move southwest, acting just as all of the others are doing. I don't know how many men Rose and Lily have available, but they won't be able to concentrate any substantial force at one particular spot if they have a whole series of movements to scout."

"Sounds reasonable," Merritt agreed. "We can use a bit of action now; it'll keep the men from going stale. Maybe they'll even learn something about campaigning in this burned-up country."

"It'll be good training, sir. This part of the country is a lot different from Virginia or the Mississippi."

"So I would judge. Now go on with your plan. Where do you propose to pick up those wagons?"

"Do you have a map handy, sir?"

The General produced one without hesitancy and Starke pointed out his landmarks as he spoke. "One wagon train — which will include the twenty wagons we are talking about — should move straight out toward Del Rio. A full battalion should be the convoy, I would judge. Allow a full week for such a column to reach Del Rio. It'll require a haul of better than twenty miles a day, but we don't want this particular column to lag."

"Will the terrain permit such a pace?"

"I think so, sir. The extra wagons will have to carry feed for the stock, however. The country's badly burnt just now and at best it's not good grazing country. Horses get mighty puny on this kind of grass."

Merritt nodded. "I'll issue orders about the matter."

"One day's march east of Del Rio the column should swing into the northeast, passing the town at a safe distance. At the first halt after passing the town the column should split, leaving the Juarez wagons and their escort to move on into the west while the remainder of the command creates a diversion by moving straight back into Del Rio. I'm in hopes that any scouts of the enemy won't notice the difference."

"Still sounds all right. Go on."

"Three days after the split the Juarez wagons ought to reach this spot here." He pointed to a bend of the Rio Grande. "They will find the ford that is marked on this map, but it will be guarded by Imperial troops. However, there is another ford about two miles upstream which the Imperials have learned to ignore. It's in the edge of the hill country and Imperial patrols don't like to go in there. Too many of them haven't gotten out again."

"Then you are planning to use the secret crossing?"

"Yes, sir. It's treacherous, but I've used it many times before."

"That's your affair. All I want to know is what we can do for you at this end."

102

"Thank you, sir. Just give me the time I've outlined and we'll make it. When do you propose to start the general movement?"

"The men are on a war footing; they should be ready to move at a moment's notice."

Starke grinned. "We don't need to be that hasty. I need time to get across and round up the men I'll need. Today is September thirtieth. Will it be convenient to order your movement for the morning of October third?"

"Perfectly."

"Then I'll get out of camp tonight. If you don't hear a report of my murder from San Antonio you'll know that the schedule is starting to work."

CHAPTER
NINE

They spent a little time on details, particularly the part about the meeting west of Del Rio. On that score Starke tried to be precise. "This will be the crucial point of the whole proceeding," he said. "Particularly if the enemy has spotted the train for what it really is. We must assume that it will be under some sort of observation, so the transfer will have to be made with due care."

"It's your program at that stage," Merritt assured him. "You give the orders."

"Very well, sir. The twenty wagons should arrive at this point east of the private ford some time on the fourteenth of October. That timing can be very important. There's a ridge at about this point . . ." He put a fingernail indentation into the map on the north side of the Rio Grande. ". . . a ridge which serves as a sort of screen. The escort should go into camp behind this ridge on the night of the fourteenth. In case they are scouted, they should make the camp appear casual, just like every other one. At about ten o'clock in the evening, however, the escort should slip away as quietly as possible, trying to avoid detection from the Mexican forces along the river. My men will move in and take the wagons at once, shoving them across the upper ford by night. In case of formal inquiry, your commander will know nothing except that he left the wagons at a particular spot and the wagons were stolen while he had his entire patrol on a night scout."

"You're risking a lot on evading observation, mister. What happens to you if the guerrillas are in strength? After our men leave, I mean."

"That's the risk I take. Naturally, your troopers will not leave the spot if it appears that the enemy is waiting in force for a seizure of the wagons. Adequate scouting will take care of that, I think."

"You seem to have it all worked out," General Merritt said quietly. "We'll handle our end. Good luck — and don't forget that this shipment is the crucial one, probably the key to all future aid. Without these supplies it is unlikely that Juarez can muster enough men to handle future shipments."

"I understand, sir. That's why I ask you to remember the need for complete secrecy. I know it will be difficult to have the dummy wagon trains acting as real decoys when their commanders don't know what they're doing, but I don't think we can take anyone else into the secret. There are too many leaks now."

"I understand," Merritt said briefly. Starke could only hope that the Mallory-Rose situation was meant.

That afternoon the details were reviewed once more with Captain Ritchie. The burly officer was affable enough now and Starke felt mildly satisfied to have him in charge. In action Ritchie would probably be all right. Only in camp was he inclined to become stuffy.

One additional detail of planning was supplied by Colonel Haney, a method of getting Starke out of camp. It was simple enough. Starke was to get some sleep early in the night and then join the officer of the guard for the change of sentries just before dawn. In that manner he could move through the guard lines until he was at the edge of camp, then simply drift away in the darkness to take his chances with whatever pickets the enemy might have posted.

At that point of planning, everything seemed satisfactory, but before the final conference could break up there was an interruption. Susan Mallory appeared outside of Colonel Haney's tent, her gay greeting sounding just a trifle forced. Starke saw Ritchie's quick frown of disapproval, but he moved out at once.

"Light down and set a spell, ma'am," he invited, putting plenty of Texas into the drawl. "It's too dad-blamed hot to be rawhidin' that bronc around this afternoon."

He gave her a hand and helped her from the saddle, one flash of the blue eyes telling him that he had not guessed wrong in thinking that her appearance had a purpose. Colonel Haney took the cue and invited her to try the water in a huge Mexican water jar he had acquired. Only Ritchie did not seem capable of putting on a show of casual cordiality.

Miss Mallory took a drink from the gourd that went with the water jar, using the movement to survey the company street behind her. Only then did she turn to face Starke. "I thought you'd like to know that Robert

Rose has been in camp. He came in with a supply train under guard, according to orders."

"Thanks," Starke said quietly. "You're just the sort of scout we need around here. Did he talk about the new guard regulations?"

"Quite strongly. He wanted my father to provide him with some sort of pass so that he could come and go without calling an escort every time. He insisted that it would be impossible to provision this camp if every food train had to proceed under guard."

Starke grinned. "I'm glad to hear it bothers him. Any discomfort for the enemy is fine with me."

Ritchie cut in rather anxiously. "Your father didn't offer him any help, did he?"

Miss Mallory's smile was one of quiet satisfaction. "My father was quite abrupt with him. He reminded him that larger armies were supplied under restricted conditions all during the war. The hint seemed clear that if Rose couldn't handle guarded shipments, some other contractor could take his place."

"Splendid," Starke approved. "Sounds like your father has had a change of heart."

She shook her head, her smile just a trifle awry. "Not that. He simply doesn't know what the new rules mean and he's putting up a big front to hide his own lack of knowledge. I'm afraid he still thinks Rose is an honest man."

"You're quite a penetrating observer," Colonel Haney remarked. "I think Mr. Starke did well in enlisting you on our side. Incidentally, may I congratulate you on your performance of last evening?"

There was a smothered grunt from Ritchie, but no one paid any attention to him. Miss Mallory glanced briefly at Starke but aimed her words at Colonel Haney. "Since I performed so well in the first act, don't you think I deserve to hear about the last act?"

"Meaning what?"

"Don't temporize, Colonel. There is a rumor in the camp that an attempt was made to ambush Lieutenant Starke last evening. I might add that Mr. Rose mentioned the rumor — without getting any information from us. I think I ought to know what happened."

"The subject is not open to discussion," Ritchie said stiffly.

"Come now, Captain," Starke murmured. "Miss Mallory's request is no more than reasonable — coming from a valuable ally. It's only fair to tell her that her old friend Eli was left behind by his friends for the noble purpose of getting rid of one Starke. Eli failed to survive."

She stared at him quietly. "You suspected something of the sort last night?" she asked.

"It seemed like a possibility."

"But you made it all sound so — silly. I'm sure I would have been all aflutter if I had known."

Starke shook his head. "I can't quite believe it. You seem to be able to take whatever comes along. Incidentally, I'd like to add my thanks to that of Colonel Haney. You helped immensely."

"But let's have no more of it!" Ritchie cut in. He had been muttering unhappily throughout the conversation.

"This is no pink tea. You've got no business meddling in anything so deadly."

She turned to study him with cool detachment. "The bullying tone doesn't become you, Ned," she said calmly. "I appreciate your interest but not to the extent of having you sound so gruff." Without giving him a chance to reply, she swung back to Starke. "It was fun helping you, Lieutenant. Maybe we'll have another opportunity some time."

Starke merely nodded. He did not trust himself to put into words what was running through his mind. After all, he was going to need the full cooperation of Captain Ritchie within the next few weeks. Better to keep quiet and get this scene over.

The rest of the day was uneventful and Starke moved across open country into San Antonio just as the first red streaks of dawn crept into the eastern sky. There had been no sign of an enemy picket outside of the army camp, but Starke did not let the fact affect him as he moved through the lanes and alleys toward the cantina of old Manuel. The danger was never absent, and just now he was doing something that could be dangerous to others as well as to himself. His very presence at the cantina would spell trouble for his hosts if the enemy were to learn of it.

The half light of dawn was adding peril to the occasion when he crept in through an unbolted back door and listened briefly to a series of snores which came from various other rooms. No one awoke to challenge him, so he moved into a smaller room, which seemed to be a sort of pantry, and stretched out on the floor, willing to catch up on some of the sleep which the restless early hours had not brought him.

Sunlight was streaming in through a high window when he was awakened by a hard blow in the ribs and a heavier one on the head and shoulder. He rolled swiftly, instinctively, and looked up to see a skillet swinging for another blow at his head. Long training stood him in good stead and he managed to take the blow on the shoulder, grabbing for the wrist of the girl who was doing the swinging.

"Lirio!" he exclaimed. "What's the idea? Don't . . ."

The immense dark eyes widened. "Señor Starke!" she gasped. "I did not recognize you. I thought a . . ."

He glanced down at the dusty garb he had donned before leaving camp. ". . . thought a beggar had crept in here to sleep, I take it. Not much reason to blame you. You play real rough, don't you?"

Her surprise and alarm faded quickly and a smile replaced the look of consternation. "With Serranio Starke I would not play so rough," she stated, her tone openly challenging. "You will stay to see?"

He studied her for a moment, his eyes narrowing a little. "I take it Diego is not here," he said flatly.

She shook her head, the smile now conspiratorial. "Yesterday he left. No one knows when he will return. Perhaps not until next week. Perhaps tonight. With Diego that is always the trouble."

Starke looked her squarely in the eyes. "Listen carefully, Lirio. Diego Menendez is one of my best friends. To me you're his girl. He trusts you — many ways. Better see to it that it stays that way."

110

A voice came from an open doorway, its Spanish quiet but a bit on the gruff side. "Always the weakness in a man's armor is the woman. I must warn Diego."

The girl swung with a mixture of pleading and imprecation. Starke saw that she was addressing a lean, tight-lipped man of perhaps thirty, a Mexican whose angry eyes were somehow impersonal in their appraisal of Lirio. Starke recognized him at once, having worked with him on a number of occasions. Pedro Valdez had suffered pretty harshly at the hands of the Clerical rebels against President Juarez, and even more so when the Imperials came in to supplant them. With him the fight to put Juarez back into the Mexican presidency was a rather personal matter. He was out to injure the people who had killed members of his family and stolen family property. He was a fanatic but a smart fighter and an excellent hand at ferreting out information about enemy troop movements. Starke suspected that Valdez might use harsh methods in making enemy soldiers talk, but he didn't care to inquire. Valdez was useful. That was enough in this war.

"Better not stir up any trouble, Pedro," Starke counseled. "I'm afraid Lirio got ideas when she saw how much of a success she was at the army dance. This morning we take time to warn her about such ideas. Then all will be well and we do not speak to Diego. Right, Lirio?"

She had turned sullen even before he spoke, but she seemed to recognize the hard threat behind the mild words. Still grasping the skillet, she swung away toward another room. "It is as you say, señores," she agreed.

"More trouble," Valdez grumbled. "I still think we should tell Diego."

"As you will," Starke said indifferently. "I believe she's still loyal in her own petty way. Now tell me of the news from below the border. Has something happened that Diego has gone away?"

"Something is about to happen. Something serious. Maximilian has decided to declare the *Ley Marcial*. It is to be put into effect on the fifteenth of next month, sooner if troops can be placed to enforce it."

"Why?" Starke inquired. "That won't make any difference to us. Our men have never been in a position to expect formal trials when caught. Martial law won't alter matters a bit."

"The move is calculated to separate us from our more timid compatriots," Valdez explained. "The Imperials think it will bring our people out of hiding. Anyone not reporting to an army post by the fifteenth is subject to being shot on sight."

"Maybe we'll have a counter-move," Starke told him. "Twenty wagons of arms and supplies ought to put courage into our party. We'll fight fire with fire."

"To you it makes no difference," Valdez said. "Nor to me. Our lives are forfeit any time we are caught. But a part of the *Ley Marcial* is to be harsh enforcement with the aid of Texas mercenaries. Many of your former rebels have been hired to patrol the border. They will receive pay and plunder. The Imperials thus hope to use the Texans as a bulwark between the United States and Mexico, freeing Imperial troops for the dirty work

112

of stamping out all opposition to the crown. That is not so good, eh?"

Starke did not bother to make the obvious reply. If the Imperial plan went into effect promptly it would add immense difficulties to the task of getting those wagons to the Juarez hideout. With only Imperial patrols to dodge, the task would not have been particularly complicated; with seasoned guerrillas patrolling the border it would be another story.

During the morning Starke found nothing in the news to make him any less sober about his prospects. Old Manuel and his sons were full of information about the guerrilla organization, stating firmly that it now numbered at least two thousand former Confederate soldiers in and around San Antonio. Similar organizations existed in other towns and cities near the border, some of the detachments already operating in full conjunction with rebel groups who had actually crossed into Mexico. Obviously the movement was on a scale that would mean plenty of trouble along the border.

CHAPTER
TEN

Within the next week Starke was to find his fears all too well grounded. In company with Valdez and Diego he worked to the southwest, crossing into Mexico without incident. Everywhere patrols of Texans guarded the border while Imperial troops swaggered in the towns and villages. If the French government proposed to take any hints from the United States Diplomatic Service they certainly were not showing any signs of it yet. Everywhere the indications were that the Maximilian government was tightening its hold on the unhappy country.

Four days out of San Antonio, Valdez swung off to the south, aiming toward Monterey in hopes of picking up information as to the number of Texans who had been enlisted. Meanwhile, Diego and Starke were to strike directly for the Juarez headquarters in the Serranias del Burro where they would gather the necessary force to pick up the shipment of arms and uniforms. Valdez would recruit also, bringing his men to the transfer point on the stated date.

"I worry about Valdez," Diego said once. "I think the man is mad. Always he goes to hunt trouble. He cannot forget that his father and his uncle were killed by the Imperials."

"He's a useful man," Starke said shortly.

"So far he has been. Always I fear that his anger will make him foolish and thus dangerous."

Starke grinned thinly. "Dangerous to the enemy, perhaps. We must take our allies for better or worse. If they are brave that is good. If anger substitutes for bravery, that is almost as good."

Diego swung in the saddle to aim a quizzical glance at him. "Are you quoting?" he asked. "It sounds almost like something our good Cervantes might have said."

"Mine," Starke insisted. "Maybe not good, but I mean it."

"Perhaps you are right. I might mention that Cervantes wrote along the same line. 'The brave man carves out his fortune, and every man is the son of his own works.' Perhaps that could be adapted to your thoughts."

"Forget the literary angles," Starke advised. "We'll not run those wagons into the Serranias on quotations."

Diego sighed. "Very well. We talk stern realities. Have you any changes in orders?"

"None. We'll divide as arranged. Circulate through the Juarista villages to the south and I'll take the more northerly camps. We meet on the evening of October fourteenth, ready to cross the river and pick up the wagon trains. If you arrive ahead of me send out scouts. I'll do the same. We'll want to know the location of all border patrols, both regular and guerrilla. Bring as many men as you can trust, but don't bring them unless they're armed. Wagon drivers must be ready to do their share of fighting."

"Understood," Diego grunted. "And don't worry about getting too many men. That *Ley Marcial* will scare off all of the timid ones."

Starke soon discovered that such was the case. He quickly lined up a dozen of his veteran followers, but it was only with difficulty that he recruited three new men. He could only hope that Diego would do better. They would need at least twenty drivers, plus armed escorts.

It was an hour past dusk on the evening of the fourteenth when Starke climbed to the top of a low knoll which had often served him in the past. From its flat top he had watched Confederate scouts and Imperial patrols on many occasions. Tonight there were no enemy units to be seen, only a misty streak which marked the trickle of wet sand that was the Rio Grande. The long days of heat had turned the river into no river at all.

Oddly enough, Starke thought, as he sat his bronc in the gloom, the river was quite a dignified stream at night. By day there was nothing but a trough of wet sand, but at night the mists hung along the trough in a winding, twisting roll that seemed quite impressive.

Making certain that he was not a silhouette against the stars, he waited long enough to study the mist streak with due care, trying to decide whether or not there might be enemy scouts along the river. His own patrols had been sent out even before nightfall and he would soon be getting their reports, but he liked to make his own observations, too. A smart man could often spot the little things which scouts sometimes missed.

Fires twinkled in the edge of the river mist at a distance of perhaps two miles and he knew that this would be the regular Imperial patrol at the ford. That one was always guarded. Only this one here in the hill country was conveniently ignored by the Imperials.

Starke chuckled mirthlessly in the darkness. He had spent quite a bit of time and effort in getting the French mercenaries to stay away from his private ford. Too bad the Texans were drawing cards. Maybe they wouldn't play the game so well.

But this was no time to be funny, he realized. Rose's guerrillas were tough, seasoned campaigners, accustomed to border warfare. They wouldn't lose any time in trying to control a spot such as the secret ford.

A shadow moved on the slope below him and Starke challenged softly but sharply in Spanish. The stranger replied in the same language, identifying himself as the scout who had been sent east to watch the approach of Ritchie's wagons.

"Have they reached the camping spot?" Starke asked.

"No, *Capitan*. They do not come tonight at all."

"You mean they didn't move from Prairie Wells today?"

"No, *Capitan*. They remain as they were last night."

"That's odd. Ritchie had only about half a day's march to reach the exchange spot. Were any other forces in the area? Anything to hint at why the wagons did not come forward?"

"I see nothing, *Capitan*. There is only the guard at the ford. Those men we do not count."

Starke chuckled at the man's scorn for the Imperials, but his tone was urgent as he asked, "Any sign of Pedro or Diego?"

"None, *Capitan*."

As though to deny the statement, there was a flurry of hoof-beats on the lower slope and voices challenged hoarsely. Starke could hear enough to realize that Diego had arrived and was having trouble with the sentries, who apparently were new men and did not know him.

"Hold everything!" Starke called. "I'll be right down."

Presently he could make out the forms of eight mounted men in the darkness. They were sitting their horses rigidly, obviously apprehensive about the two guards who menaced them with rifles.

"Your sentinels are hard men," Diego observed calmly in Spanish. "Alert but forbidding. Have the kindness to tell them to lower their gun hammers carefully. Accidental bullets are just as dangerous as the other kind."

Starke smiled briefly and called an order to his men. "Back to your posts, men. You have done well, but this is not the enemy. Lieutenant Diego has arrived with reinforcements."

He turned quickly to Diego. "Have you seen anything of Ritchie? Tonight we were to meet him at the agreed place. My scout tells me he has not moved from Prairie Wells."

"Your scout is correct. My men have been scouting his column since he left the other part of his force at Del Rio. He was on schedule at Prairie Wells but fortified his camp after a night raid that was nothing but a demonstration."

"A raid? I hadn't heard of that! Who raided?"

"That we do not know. My men could not cover every point. The raiders came from the east and probably were from the Texas force that was tailing him."

"How big an outfit was this? The Texans, I mean."

"Six men. Scouts, I think."

"And you have some idea what they were up to?"

"I make a guess, my friend. I think the Texas scouts finally decide that the wagons they trail are the ones their commander wants to find. They call upon their allies across the border and feint an attack in order to halt Captain Ritchie's march. Meanwhile, one of their number is riding hard to report."

"And Ritchie fell for the trick?"

"It would appear so."

Neither man bothered to put the next thought into words. Obviously, the enemy wanted to have an overwhelming force on hand for the moment when the regular troops would turn over the wagons to the representatives of the Juarez forces. They proposed to do some hijacking with plenty of men.

"Seen anything of Pedro?" Starke asked.

"No."

"We could use him. I hope he gets here pretty soon."

"Then you propose a move?"

"Of course. We've got to make our move before the Texans can get their full forces here. How many men did you bring?"

"Seven."

"And I have twenty. Scarcely enough for a decent picket. Not anywhere near what we ought to have for a running fight of any sort. We'll need most of our crew to drive the wagons."

"Then you think we can get them away before the fight starts? The wagons, I mean."

"There's a chance. We'll have to take it. Felipe! Are you still here?"

The scout's voice came excitedly. *"Si, Capitan."*

"Gather the others. Pass the word that every man is to concentrate here and take orders from Lieutenant Diego. When all are accounted for, you are to cross at the ford and move eastward on the American side. Move cautiously, but don't waste time. I'm heading for Ritchie's camp right away."

"A moment, my friend," Diego interposed. "You propose to make the movement of the wagons tonight?"

"If possible. From here it is but half a day's wagon march to Prairie Wells. Perhaps slightly more, but no matter. Riding light, we can make it in three hours. That puts me in Ritchie's camp an hour before midnight. By midnight you and the men should be there, also. If the exchange can be made we could be back at the ford only slightly after daybreak."

"You would cross in daylight?"

"Better to cross in daylight without opposition than to fight across in the dark with Rose's guerrillas at our heels."

"Very well. But be careful. Enemy scouts will be watching their camp."

Even in the low-hanging mists Starke made his way quickly and confidently across the wet sands that would be river bottom when the rainy season came. The path required much twisting and turning to avoid patches of quicksand, but Starke did not delay. This had been the path for some of his most hazardous raids, as well as for a couple of hard-pressed retreats. He knew it so well that few men ventured to follow him across it unless he wished them to. In the past both French and Confederate troops had drawn back from the venture.

He glanced at the stars as he emerged from the river mists, estimating the time to be still some minutes short of eight thirty. Then he put spurs to his bronc and lined out toward Prairie Wells and the laggard Ritchie. In his brief conversation with Diego he had made himself sound cheerful, but now he had no reason to keep up the front. It was all too clear that a plan which depended largely upon careful timing was already hopelessly off schedule. By this time the Texans would know the score and would be driving to catch up with the quarry that had eluded them briefly. Every minute of further delay would narrow that slim margin of safety.

There was no sign of life on the Texas side of the Rio Grande and Starke pushed forward at a good pace, spurring the bronc in the open stretches and walking him through the breaks in the low ridges. This was the mile-eating pace of the regular cavalry, particularly well suited to the present conditions. The lights of the Imperial outpost fell behind and within ten minutes he had passed the spot where Ritchie's column should have been. No one moved anywhere in the series of hollows behind the screening ridge.

He kept his mount at the same pace for nearly two hours, a sense of position rather than actual sight warning him that he was closing in on Prairie Wells. That meant danger, since Ritchie's camp almost certainly was under enemy surveillance.

Slowing the pace a little, he considered the situation with some care. Ritchie had probably halted for a bigger reason than those reported demonstrations. That reason might mean added danger. Maybe the enemy knew of the planned meeting places. In that case they would know something of Starke's plans. All the more reason to proceed with caution.

Suddenly he made out the low escarpment which marked the western approach to the series of water holes where Ritchie's half company was supposed to be in camp. He dismounted at the foot of the slope, climbing the rise with caution, alert to every tiny sound of the night. It seemed likely that enemy scouts would be posted along this break, but presently he could see the dying fires of a camp and nowhere could he detect the presence of an enemy.

He studied the camp with the minute attention to detail which had become almost second nature to him. Two circles of fires, which were already reduced to mere glows: one would be the wagon camp, and the other the cooking fires of the troopers. A little to one side a larger fire still shone brightly and around it he could make out the forms of several men, firelight twinkling on buttons and braid.

"Ritchie must think he's on parade," Starke growled under his breath. "I thought he'd know better than to ride out here in dress uniform."

He moved the horse across the slope a little distance, picketing him where he would not be silhouetted too much against the starlit sky. Then he moved toward the camp, using every clump of mesquite just as a Comanche might have done. Maybe so much precaution was not necessary, but after three years of this sort of thing a man developed habits. One of Starke's best habits was to take no chances with unknown situations. He wanted to know a lot more about Ritchie's situation before he disclosed himself.

The sentinels were easy to spot and he evaded them with practiced ease. When a man has learned to be elaborately careful about such tiny matters as the squeak of a gun against leather, dodging pickets who are neither alert nor experienced is reasonably simple.

He paused long enough to listen to the muttered exchange of words between two sentries, realizing that the men were uneasy about something but not especially worried about any threat from outside. Then he got a closer glimpse of the uniforms by the fire and began to understand. Ritchie was there — garbed like a real campaigner, Starke noted with satisfaction — but two strange officers were with him. The larger one, a sturdy-looking, middle-aged man with a heavy mustache, wore the shoulder insignia of a major, while the yellow stripe on his leg marked him as a cavalryman. He seemed amiably at ease, chatting with Ritchie, while a lean-faced younger man in the uniform of a cavalry lieutenant sat back in dour silence.

Starke could not get close enough to overhear the talk, but the major seemed to be doing more than his share of it. Ritchie was clearly uneasy, worried.

Then Starke stood up, walking calmly toward the trio without anyone seeming to notice. He overheard a fragment of talk about the rival Mexican leaders in which the major flatly declared, "We can't trust any of them," and then Ritchie jumped up with an exclamation of surprise.

"Where did you come from?" he snapped.

"From up the river," Starke told him. "From the spot where this column was supposed to be." He purposely ignored the other officers but did not fail to see the swift exchange of glances between them. Both of them were complete strangers to him.

"Sorry about missing connections," Ritchie said, his face a little red. "As you'll soon see, I had no choice in the matter. Colonel Haney apparently received some new orders after we left San Antonio and he sent me word to halt at this point. Major Weldon and Lieutenant Brant came in last night with orders to that effect."

He swung to face the older man. "Major Weldon, this is Lieutenant Starke, the officer to whom I was ordered to deliver the wagons. Will you be so kind as to explain the matter to him, sir?"

Starke saluted in recognition of the introduction, tipping a somewhat less formal gesture to the lean lieutenant in the rear. Major Weldon remained seated, looking formal and sounding rather pompous as he remarked, "I presume you will be annoyed at the alteration of plans, Lieutenant, but this is a most delicate matter. Our State Department concluded that it would be most unwise to risk an overt act against the present Mexican authority. The entire proposition has been canceled and a new plan has been substituted."

"May I inquire, sir, as to the alternate plan?" Starke forced himself to adopt a tone as formal as the major's. He even managed to approximate the other man's overly precise enunciation.

"Naturally, Lieutenant. Your cooperation becomes an integral part of the new plan. I am sure you are aware that there are now in Mexico at least four major revolutionary groups, each led by a man who hopes to become dictator of the country by overthrowing the present government. Each hopes to receive aid from the United States. Correct?"

"Substantially," Starke said. "I'm a bit prejudiced, I suppose, but I don't lump all of the Mexican leaders as dictator prospects. Santa Anna and Diaz probably yes. Juarez simply wants to regain the lawful presidency from which he was driven. Escobeda's ambitions are dubious; he appears now as a real supporter of Juarez."

The major waved a hand carelessly. "We will not quibble about terms. The important thing is that there

125

exists a rivalry between leaders. Our own position would be embarrassing if we were to commit ourselves to aiding the wrong group, at the same time antagonizing a European power. So we must move with caution and careful diplomacy." Again Starke had a feeling that the words were being pronounced a little too carefully. Major Weldon would have been extremely pompous even without that mustache.

"I can see that, sir," he said quietly. "So what do we do with the wagons? Haul them back to San Antone?"

"Not yet, Lieutenant. The time of real decision has not yet arrived. Our backing must be withheld until we are certain that we are betting on the proper group. Then we must be ready to give assistance without delay."

"Colonel Haney seemed to be pretty certain that Juarez was our man."

Major Weldon's smile was a trifle supercilious. "Colonel Haney is merely an undercover agent in the field. He does not make decisions. Diplomatic requirements frequently necessitate overruling him."

"Likely enough. However, I'm interested just now in where this leaves me."

"I have your orders, Lieutenant. Your men are available, of course?"

"Yes, sir."

"You will order them back across the Rio Grande, making some show of the movement in order that it becomes clear to the Mexican authorities that they are carrying no supplies with them. At the same time, Captain Ritchie and his men will retire toward San

Antonio, leaving the wagons here for a detachment which has been sent out to pick them up and move them to a place where they will be placed under guard until the proper moment arrives."

"Proper moment? For what?"

"Who knows? That is up to the State Department. Meanwhile, the supplies will be under guard of a force which does not even appear to be part of the army. In that way we disclose nothing to any scouts from across the Rio Grande."

"But you will be in command of that force, sir?"

"For the time being. My men should be here within the next twelve hours." He seemed to unbend a little as he added with a smile, "You may be interested to know, Lieutenant, that my command will be made up of what are referred to in the ranks as galvanized Yankees, former Confederate prisoners who have volunteered for irregular duty with our army. They know the country and can give the project full security without anything official entering into the picture. Lieutenant Brant and I will not even appear in uniform after taking charge of the group."

Ritchie broke in then, his voice somewhat subdued. "My men are rolling out an hour before dawn, Starke. We'll slip away then to avoid observation. Major Weldon, Lieutenant Brant, and the two enlisted men who came with them will look after the wagons until the balance of the force arrives."

Starke looked up quickly, wondering at the remark. It seemed almost as though Ritchie had wanted to mention those two enlisted men. Was it possible that

127

Ritchie was entertaining any doubts of Major Weldon? If such was the case the big cavalryman didn't show any sign of it in his expression or attitude.

"One other matter, Lieutenant," Weldon went on. "With affairs changing so rapidly, it may be necessary to bring your company into action again. If we need you, how do we find you? How would it do for you to furnish us with instructions and a password for reaching the Juarez stronghold?"

"Sorry, sir. It's not my secret to reveal."

"You are under orders, Lieutenant. Your duty is to your government, not to a foreign bandit chieftain."

Starke shook his head. "My orders, sir, and my peculiar type of duty demands that I make certain decisions for myself. At this point I feel that I should not reveal the information you request. If I change my mind I'll let you know before I leave." He turned abruptly to Ritchie, fully aware of the flat silence which greeted this calm disregard of authority. "Any grub handy, Captain? I skipped supper tonight."

Major Weldon seemed about to protest, but he stifled his anger with an obvious effort and turned away. Starke waited for a moment, then turned to follow Ritchie, who had started toward the nearest wagon without making any comment.

CHAPTER
ELEVEN

Starke glanced back once to see Weldon and Brant in a close conference. Then Ritchie muttered in his ear, "You're shoving your neck out, Starke. That Weldon acts like a martinet to me."

"Doesn't he act like anything else?"

"What do you mean?"

"I think you know. Just in case you won't admit it, I'll tell you that I think he's a faker. I propose to call his bluff."

"How? If he's real he's the senior officer here. He can make a lot of trouble for either one of us."

"I'm betting he's not real."

Ritchie risked a little louder reply as they drew away from the fire. "I stirred up enough hard feeling when I insisted on seeing his credentials. They're all in order. He was a captain in Phil Kearney's corps. Promoted to major after Fredericksburg and transferred to undercover operations when Grant took command. I'm afraid he's what he claims to be."

"Where are the two enlisted men?"

"Under that second wagon — asleep. They didn't seem to feel very sociable toward my boys."

"Under orders, I'll bet. Is Sergeant McCall with you?"

"Sure. He'll be at the commissary wagon."

They found McCall as predicted and the lanky noncom saluted with a smartness that did not match his friendly grin. "Looks like we got complications, sir," he observed to Starke.

"Real complications maybe," Starke told him, biting at a bit of hardtack. "Let me repeat what I've just been telling Captain Ritchie. I think Weldon is an agent of the Maximilian forces. He's trying to hoax us into giving up the munitions without a fight. At worst, he hopes to keep us dillydallying long enough to let Rose and Lily come up with their guerrillas."

"I still think his papers are all right," Ritchie insisted.

"Likely they were. The Confederate army must have captured thousands of sets of perfectly good identification papers. At any rate, the French are good at that sort of thing; they'd be able to forge any kind of papers they want. I pick Weldon to be an educated foreign mercenary, probably a German, who is playing this role to keep Juarez from getting those muskets."

"But I . . ." Ritchie began.

"I understand. Your career would be ruined if you acted on my hunch and it turned out to be wrong. So I'm going to take it right out of your hands. All I ask is that you don't try to get heroic when I start operating."

"What do you propose to do?"

"Capture this camp. Actually, I think I could do it anyway — but that's not the point. We don't want to be fighting our own allies. When I make my move you'll be covered by a gun of some sort. Just take it easy. Understand?"

"I'm afraid I don't. This sounds like . . ."

Starke interrupted again. "Sergeant McCall, I'm depending on you for something a little more difficult. You've got to play both ways. I'll have men in camp who will serve as the capturing force, but they won't know about Weldon's men. I want you to pick three good men and have them ready to cover Weldon and his boys when the fun begins. No shooting if we can avoid it. Also, try to pass the word to the other men that they are to make no show of resistance to me or my command."

"See here, Starke," Ritchie protested. "You're being pretty high-handed about all this. I don't . . ."

"I'm protecting you," Starke told him. "If I fail, I'm just an outlaw who dared to hold up an army detachment. That's why McCall and his boys will have to be careful how they carry out their end of the deal. You can give them some kind of an out later if things go wrong. However, I propose to have these wagons out of here within the hour, one way or another."

"You talk as though you had help. Where are your men?"

"That's another thing, Captain. If you're going to campaign on this border you'd better start learning a few things and seeing that your men do the same. Did anyone see me come into this camp tonight?"

"No, I suppose not. Suddenly you were there and I forgot to ask about the lack of any challenge."

"One of the things you can't afford to forget. I came in unchallenged because your sentries don't know that regulations don't mean much down here. You don't guard a camp by standing up and making yourself into a target. Evading your picket line was no trouble. What I did, others can do. Unless I am mistaken about a couple of night-bird cries that I just heard, you are already invaded. I'll bet I've got twenty men inside your picket line at this moment."

"Are you serious?"

"Completely. Hustle along, McCall, and get your men placed. In five minutes I'm going to demand the surrender of this camp. Make sure that you seem properly astonished when I call the turn."

He moved away before Ritchie could argue.

Starke saw that Ritchie was going slowly back toward the two questionable officers. He also noted that most of the men in camp were restless and awake. Evidently they had been alert to the fact that something had gone wrong. He hoped that McCall would pass the word so that no shooting would start.

The five-minute time interval was almost over when he saw a pair of troopers shift their positions to a point nearer one of the wagons. The men seemed to be rolling in their blankets, but he saw that both kept carbines in their hands. They would be able to take care of the two men under the wagon.

He moved slowly across toward the west end of the camp, speaking to men he had learned to know by sight. The move permitted him to receive a stealthy sign from Diego. The entire force of Mexicans had moved in, not quite knowing what to do but trusting their superior to put them in a position of the most use.

"Disregard the regular troops," he said aloud, apparently speaking to the night in general. "Watch me and take your cue."

Then he strode back to where Ritchie was talking earnestly to Major Weldon. "I've made up my mind, Major," he announced. "I refuse to give any information about Juarez."

"Insubordination!" the heavy man snapped. "Do you realize what it means?"

"Of course. It means that I don't think you're Major Weldon at all. And don't reach for a weapon. My men have you covered. In fact, we have the entire camp covered." He raised his voice. "Diego! Deploy three men to guard each rack of carbines. Keep the rest under cover as they are."

Out of the corner of his eye he could see some of his command appear as though by magic. Almost instantly armed men were standing at strategic spots all through the camp. He noted with satisfaction that the troopers who had rolled their carbines in their blankets were lying quite still. So far so good.

"Are you out of your mind, Lieutenant?" Weldon stormed. "This is mutiny! It's treason!"

"There are nasty names for what *you* are doing," Starke told him. "Captain Ritchie, you will please refrain from giving any foolish orders to your men. As you can plainly see, I have this camp surrounded." He could only hope that McCall had reached enough of the men so that none of them would try to do anything foolishly heroic. One shot now might start a bloody row.

"Seize him, men!" Weldon shouted. "This is an order!"

"Ignore him, men," Starke called. "He's not an officer at all but an enemy agent in disguise."

He purposely kept his tone loud enough for the nearer men to hear as he swung back to Weldon. "It was a smart trick, mister whatever-your-name-is, but it just won't work. Did you hope to get us to turn these munitions over to the Imperials directly, or were you just hoping to make a delay until Rose's gang could catch up?"

The older man's gaze wavered for an instant. Starke plunged ahead. "I suppose you won't talk, but it's one of three things. In any event, Juarez didn't get his guns. Now the problem is what we are to do with you. Undoubtedly the Juarez folks would be delighted to keep you for a pet. If they hold a few important hostages perhaps they can persuade your side to stop some of its butchery."

"You can't do this, Starke!" Ritchie exclaimed. "Don't you realize what it will mean to you if you send these men across into Mexico?"

"I've got an idea what it'll mean to them," Starke replied grimly. "However, I'll make you an offer. If you'll consider this fellow as the impostor I'm sure he is, I'll turn him over to you as a prisoner. You can take him back and let him stand trial for impersonating an officer."

"But I . . ."

134

"Yes, I know. You're afraid he's not the fake I claim him to be. In which case you're in a mess. Maybe it'll be better to do it my way. We'll let the Juarez people handle him and then nobody will make any charges against you."

A man came forward out of the gloom and Starke realized that the grim Pedro had arrived in time to take part in this fantastic bit of acting. At the moment Pedro seemed entirely serious. He stared fixedly at Major Weldon and then turned to Starke, speaking in Spanish. "You have identified him correctly, *Capitan*. The man is an officer of the Monterey garrison. I have seen him several times."

Weldon's expression indicated that he understood the words. Starke nodded easily toward him. "We'll make it your choice, mister. You played it pretty smart, even to a little detail like assuming the identity of an officer from a foreign regiment. That would cover your slight tendency to speak English too carefully. Now maybe you'll be smart enough to know that your best bet is to make sure that Captain Ritchie accepts you as a prisoner. The United States will probably be more merciful than the Juaristas."

"Be not overly merciful," Diego cautioned in Spanish. "A hostage would be useful to our leader."

Still the burly man did not change expression. Starke thought there was a slight show of uneasiness in the eyes, but if the fellow knew Spanish he concealed his emotions well. If he did not . . .

"I offer a compromise," Starke said shortly. "As of this moment I am in command of the situation, so I take full responsibility for what I propose to do. The exchange of wagons will go forward as scheduled. After my men are on the way with them I propose to turn matters back to the control of Captain Ritchie. I have Colonel Haney's word for it that at this stage of the game I am authorized to assume such responsibility, even if my present actual control is not enough. The four men who came into this camp tonight are to be held by Captain Ritchie as prisoners until they can be identified. After that I leave matters up to others."

"And if I refuse?" Ritchie snapped.

"Then I assume another kind of responsibility. Taking the prisoners with me, I head for Mexico. One way or another, Captain, you need accept no responsibility. As for the men in your command who have aided me in this move, I trust you will recall that they were assigned to me by Colonel Haney. They are not to be held accountable for anything. That is a part of the bargain."

Ritchie glanced at the scowling Weldon and nodded his agreement. "I have no choice," he said shortly. "Please take notice that I disclaim all responsibility."

Starke did not bother to discuss the matter further. Time was important and those wagons had to be started west toward the secret ford. If he was wrong about Major Weldon he would have some unhappy explaining to do — but he didn't think he was wrong. The prisoner had seemed too content to remain in the custody of Ned Ritchie.

At any rate, he didn't let it bother him. "I'd take it as a favor, Captain, if you'd have your men give us a hand in getting those wagons ready. Time is running out and we're several miles short of where we ought to be." He didn't put any stress on the statement, but he could see the angry flush in Ritchie's glowering countenance. "By the way, sir, I hear you had some sort of demonstration against your pickets last night. Anything important?"

"False alarm," Ritchie said shortly. He swung away and began to issue the orders Starke had requested. At the same time Starke sent his own forces into action, grimly aware that Pedro and two of his men were standing guard over the prisoners. Ritchie had forgotten that detail, probably because he hadn't yet recovered from the shock of finding himself and his command such easy victims for Starke's guerrillas.

In spite of the tension, there was little confusion, and Starke felt that he could credit most of the progress to Sergeant McCall. The lanky redhead was having the time of his life doing the sort of thing a good sergeant was not supposed to do. Within a surprisingly short time the wagons were moving out in a long line and Starke was waving a wordless farewell to Ritchie.

The first pink streaks of dawn were showing behind the little wagon train when Pedro rode up to make a report. Diego had passed the word that the dour Mexican had arrived with only one other man, so that the company's strength was still dangerously low — thirty-one men to handle twenty wagons under perilous conditions. Starke had decided to gamble heavily on his guard, keeping only himself and Diego with the wagons while Pedro organized the remaining eight into vedettes.

"A man from across the river," Pedro announced abruptly. "He does not stay with us, but he brings word that the Imperials over there are warned to be alert. Texans will try to trap us on this side and none of us must be permitted to escape into Mexico."

"Any hint as to how close this Texas outfit is?"

"The message does not say. Only that they are coming fast."

"Keep your men fanned out on both sides and at the rear. I think we're safe enough in front — if we don't stumble onto a band of ambitious Comanches. If the enemy appears, send one man to warn us and then skirmish carefully. Make as much delay for us as you can, but don't lose men by exposing them too much. I've got an idea the odds are going to be pretty bad without any further reduction of force for us."

"You will cross by daylight then?"

"Under the circumstances it might be better that way. Less chance of running into an ambush. Any prospect of the Imperials throwing substantial forces in this direction?"

Pedro shrugged. "Likely they will try. To my knowledge they do not have much strength in this region."

"Good. We'll have enough trouble without them."

The Mexican rode away into the gray of the dawn, leaving Starke to consider the situation as it now appeared. Behind him he could hear the grate of hoofs against the sandy soil and the grind of wagon tires rolling against the pebbles. Sharp Latin voices yelped imprecations at the dogged mules, while whips cracked their punctuations of the Spanish curses. Twenty wagonloads of material were on the way to Juarez, material for which several parties would be cheerfully willing to do murder.

No one mentioned food. Breakfast would be eaten on the move or not eaten at all. By the first streaks of real daylight Starke inspected the mules in the train and saw to his relief that they were in good condition. Ritchie had not forced them too much and the day of rest had been helpful. The animals could be driven hard if necessary.

The sun was an hour high when they approached the chain of hills which was supposed to have marked the delivery point. Another hour would bring them to the ford. If no opposition developed in that interval the worst would be over.

Pedro rode in as though to dispel any optimism. "Felipe, my best scout, tells of a large force in the rear," he reported. "Felipe is part Indian; he reads numbers from the dust cloud." Then he added, "But Felipe likes to tell the good story and best stories have the biggest numbers."

Starke grinned quizzically. "You mean you hate to believe what he reports?"

Pedro's sour features relaxed into a wolfish grin. "It is as you say, *Capitan*. Felipe is so much the liar, but this time I think he tells only truth when he says there are fifty men on our trail."

"Very good. You left your men to skirmish as I ordered?"

"Soon you will hear the first shots."

"Good. Hold 'em for an hour and we'll know whether we can risk a crossing or fight it out on this side. I'd sure like to get into those hills on the other side of the river if we could make it."

A crackle of gunfire drifted to his ears almost as soon as Pedro rode away. It was still far to the rear and the firing was not heavy, so he contented himself with urging the drivers to greater speed. Then, when the secret ford was almost in sight, the firing stopped.

He rode back along the line until he found Diego. "Take charge here," he shouted. "Get the train down to the river, but be ready to fort up on this side. I want to know what's happening back there before we commit ourselves to the crossing."

Then he was spurring hard toward the rear. He had expected that they would have to fight a brisk rear guard action in order to get the wagons over. Now the fighting had ceased. That had to mean something and he knew better than to hope that the enemy would have withdrawn.

CHAPTER
TWELVE

Starke was scarcely clear of the wagon train's dust cloud when he saw Pedro and another Mexican coming toward him at full gallop. He did not have to ask his question.

"They divide their force," Pedro announced, pulling his bronc to a sliding halt. "Half withdraw and watch our skirmishers. The other half crosses the river at the regular ford."

"Got any idea what they're planning?"

"The obvious thing," Pedro said with an elaborate shrug. "The men who go into Mexico will join with the Imperials and try to intercept us, while those who stay on this side wait to attack our rear while our wagons are in mid-crossing."

"Sounds likely. Got any better count of the enemy?"

Again there was that slight trace of wolfish grin on the man's dark features. "Felipe was quite accurate this time. I was able to count them at my leisure. Fifty-two, counting the men who lead the extra horses."

"With probably more to come," Starke said grimly. "The report has it that Rose can command several hundred men, maybe even thousands. This will be the nearest detachment that could be turned in our direction. We'll have to fight our way through this outfit or we'll be hemmed in by larger numbers."

"There is one point of aid," Pedro said. "The leader did not withdraw soon enough. The men who cross the river had to ride back to the ford. If we are fortunate we can make the crossing before they can reach the Mexican side of our private ford. At least, we should be able to get some of our wagons across so that their drivers can defend the crossing from that side."

"We'll try," Starke told him. "You'd better make sure that you have all good riflemen with you. Once we're into the business of making the crossing you'll have to play sniper to defend our rear. You don't have enough men for any other kind of skirmishing."

"I will arrange it," Pedro assured him.

Starke knew his man well enough to feel that no further instructions were necessary. He waved a brief salute and hurried back toward the wagons, which were already beginning to wind slightly downgrade toward the stretch of wet sands which made up the river. He paused at the head of the column to pass the news to Diego.

"Handle the crossing," he ordered. "I'll go over and act as the advance scout. Tell the drivers to be alert for signals from me, but in any case to make for that first little ridge when they reach the other side of the stream. We'll fort up there if we have to."

"And if we reach the spot," Diego reminded him. "There is many a slip . . ."

"Cervantes," Starke grimaced and wheeled his bronc.

"No. It was . . ."

That part of Starke's literary education was neglected. He heard nothing but the wind in his ears and the rattle of his mount's hoofs as he rode hard for the secret ford. Still, he was grinning comfortably. It was good to have a cool customer like Diego around in a tight spot.

He crossed to the Mexican side without seeing any sign of an enemy. A glance to the rear told him that six of the wagons were already moving out from the American side, while no warning crackle of fire had sounded from the rear of the train. The enemy seemed to have made a slight mistake in geography, a mistake which was going to allow the fugitives the time they needed.

The morning sun was in his eyes when he urged his mount up the first ridge, but he could still see the moving figures downstream. A long line of riders came toward him at full gallop, their dust making it impossible for him to estimate numbers. He thought he could make out a couple of uniforms, however, so he decided that the Texas irregulars had indeed become allies of the Imperials.

"It makes them legitimate," he mused aloud. "On the other side they were rebels, outlaws, or traitors. Now they're working for the legal government. My outfit is the crowd that's beyond the law. We'll have to keep that in mind."

There was a trace of irony in his voice as he muttered the last statement. For all practical purposes it didn't make much difference how much law was on which side. This was to be a fight to the death. Either his men had to cut their way through to hill country where lurking rebels would turn out to help them or they would be wiped out mercilessly.

He calculated distances swiftly, aware that those riders on the riverbank must see the wagons at the ford. Unless one of the lead wagons should get badly bogged, he told himself, seven or eight vehicles would be on high ground before the enemy could get within gunshot. That ought to be margin enough for men who knew how to use slim chances.

He barked orders as the first wagons reached the spot where he waited. "Fort up here, men. All wagons in usual defense positions, mules to the inside. Carlos and Rodriguez, come with me and bring rifles. You other drivers take care of their outfits. Their mules won't stampede until you can take care of them; they're too tired."

Both men mentioned jumped from wagonseats and mounted horses which had been trotting behind their respective wagons. Starke nodded approval and led them east along the river to where a mesquite thicket capped a ridge that was somewhat lower than the one on which the wagons were taking position. Even as they made the move he could hear a rattle of gunshots from the American side of the Rio Grande.

"The enemy tried to time the attack so that they'd hit us from both sides at the same time," he commented. "We're just lucky that they let their timing get a bit late. Leave the broncs here behind the ridge and get ready to snipe from the mesquite. If we can bluff 'em here for ten minutes — and Pedro's boys can do the same — we'll be past the worst of it."

Both men grinned and dismounted, starting up the slope as though glad to get at something other than the business of mule driving. Starke called further instructions. "Spread out well. Carlos, you go straight up. Rodriguez, bear to the right thirty yards. I'll take the knob close to the river. Make every shot count — and don't pass up a good shot at a Texan just to have the fun of knocking down an Imperial!"

He was into the mesquite almost as he finished shouting, quickly getting a good look at the approaching attackers. They were only about two hundred yards away and riding hard along the river bank.

He found himself a spot where he could lie flat and command the whole line of approach. Diving into it without delay, he lined the sights of his Sharps on the lanky man in dusty blue who rode at the head of the attack. Even at the distance Starke recognized the fellow as an old enemy, a guerrilla who had operated along the border all during the war.

He squeezed grimly, making himself remember that he had two chores to accomplish. These attackers had to be halted and at the same time the odds needed to be shaved.

For an instant the smoke of the shot hid the target from him, but by the time he had shoved in another shell he saw that the riders were in some disorder, milling around three figures on the ground. Only then did he realize that two other shots had been fired from the ridge beside him. Evidently both Carlos and Rodriguez had done deadly work with their opening blasts.

He sighted on a man whose uniform showed gaudy red lapels, obviously a Maximilian officer. Again he scored a hit and the enemy went back in some confusion, leaving four men on the ground while four riderless horses raced off in as many directions.

"Hold your fire," Starke called. "Watch carefully. If they come on again we'll give them another dose of the same medicine. If they try to ride around us we'll get back in the saddle and move to another spot."

The confusion in the enemy ranks was lessening now. A bearded man seemed to be giving orders, well out of range, and Starke watched grimly as the distant horsemen moved in response to those new orders. This time they spread out as a line of skirmishers, ten men moving straight up the river with wide spaces between them, while the balance of the party swung wide to the south as though to make a flanking movement.

There was still an occasional shot from beyond the river, but the sound hinted that Pedro's men were holding their positions. Starke took a quick look at the ford and saw to his satisfaction that the wagon drivers were handling their work well. Fifteen wagons were safely across, most of them already in defense order.

"Back to your broncs," he yelled to his two snipers. "Keep in front of those men to the south. Don't expose yourselves if you can help it, but slow 'em down! I'll see what I can do about the others."

146

The two Mexicans raced down the ridge to their ponies and within seconds were moving in a course parallel to the enemy flankers. Starke went down on his belly again, laying four cartridges on the brim of his hat, which was already on the ground. He wanted shells handy for reloading and the hat would keep the cartridge grease from picking up sand.

Again he let the advancing men draw within decent range, picking a target with all the care in the world. This time the enemy did not let the casualties panic them. Instead, they spurred forward in a direct assault upon the ridge. Probably they thought several men were still there, but they clearly intended to take the position by storm. Not a healthy location for a single rifleman.

Starke drove in two more shots, then grabbed his hat and shells to retreat down the west slope of the ridge. He reloaded as he ran, knocking over the first man who broke the skyline. As nearly as he could determine, six of the attacking force were now killed or wounded. So far so good.

Evidently the other riders had turned cautious and Starke used the interval to move toward the wagons, leading his pony and backing up slowly so that he could keep his eyes on the mesquite. Only when he was some two hundred feet away did the first slug whine past him, announcing that the enemy had seized the sniping post. Instantly Starke leaped into the saddle and sent the pony at a dead run for the high ground where the wagons were halting.

Diego met him just short of the spot. "I've put Mendoza in charge of the defense," he reported. "He's stationing the men in defensive spots as soon as they can leave their teams."

"Good. But we'll need to be more active than that. It looks to me like that last wagon cut the final bend too short. They're bogging down. Better send four men with horses out there. Have two more take rifles and be ready to cover Pedro's retreat. He'll be breaking out from the American side any minute now."

Diego hurried to give the orders while Starke motioned to a pair of teamsters who were waiting at the near side of the wagon fort. "Work out about two hundred yards to the south. Cover Carlos and Rodriguez. They may need help. The enemy's mounted, but we'll get help to you if they try to rush you."

Almost as he spoke they could see the two mounted men retreating toward them, firing at an enemy which was still unseen. Rifle fire was also beginning to sound from the distant mesquite ridge, but Starke didn't pay too much attention. The real danger was not from such long-range fire; the defense had to set up its best guard against a headlong cavalry charge. If the enemy commander was smart he would see that this was his best bet. Such an attack would prevent the wagons from becoming a real fort.

It quickly became apparent that the guerrilla leader understood his business. There was a short conference as the knot of riders came around the south end of the ridge, and then two men rode to the higher ground and sat their horses quietly as they surveyed the scene.

148

Starke tried to think of the situation from their viewpoint. They could see a wagon train trying desperately to get into defensive position. It must be clear to them that there were few defenders except for the wagon drivers themselves and that they were now busy with several chores. Some were still trying to get the teams picketed while others were struggling to free the wagon which had edged into the quicksand. With perhaps thirty men still available, the attack must look like a mighty good bet.

Starke whistled a shrill blast. Carlos had been with him in similar skirmishes and would know what the signal meant. He could see the Mexican shouting at the others and immediately the four skirmishers started back toward the wagons.

"Get all extra weapons loaded and handy!" Starke shouted. "They'll hit us right away. Diego, keep some men on the side nearest the river to protect that outfit there. I'll handle this side."

He realized that there had been no recent firing from the American shore, but he didn't have time to consider what it meant. For the moment the real concern was the impending attack from the southeast.

For a minute or two the ridge became silent as men waited. On the river sands other men worked feverishly but in silence, so that the entire scene became slightly unreal to Starke as he studied it. Then an exchange of shouts from the mesquite indicated a decision made. The attack came a couple of additional minutes after that. The ten men who had ridden out as flankers were now aligned with the others who had stormed the mesquite ridge. Again the line was widely spaced, eight uniformed Imperial soldiers and twenty-one nondescripts who were probably Texans of the Rose-Lily guerrilla force. They came on steadily and Starke guessed that they would try the same ruse they had used on him.

"Hold your fire!" he bawled to his defenders, noting that most of them had taken positions under the wagons. Having fought cavalry from afoot on other occasions when they were retreating with stolen wagons, they knew this was the best kind of defense. "They will charge when we open fire. Let me draw the charge; you hold your fire until they've closed in a little." Starke knew he could depend on his veterans to obey that order. If some of the new men grew nervous and fired too soon, they'd merely help to draw the enemy into a premature rush.

He glanced around once to make sure that every wagoner had abandoned other chores to take up defensive posts, but he didn't stop to count heads. At best he couldn't have more than twelve men with him; it was just as well not to know the exact odds when they were so bad.

The attacking horsemen came on slowly and Starke saw that they were concentrating on his own position. He had half expected to see them split their force with the idea of trapping those men on the river sands, but the enemy commander evidently had decided to take one bite at a time. Perhaps he was even disgruntled at the way the earlier division of forces had failed. Certainly the twenty-odd men on the other side of the river were taking no very important part in the fight.

150

This was the only cheerful thought Starke could muster.

Somewhere close at hand a man swore grimly in Spanish, while another joked nervously in a high-pitched voice. Starke recalled once more that there were green men in his crew, men who might not know how to fight this kind of battle.

"Hold your positions under the wagons!" he shouted. "One round from carbines when they are within a hundred feet. Then switch to whatever side-arms you have ready. Don't try to reload your carbines; that's what they're counting on." He wished he had some of those Spencer or Henry repeaters that had been coming on the market. That kind of weapon would surely put a crimp in the plans of a cavalry commander who figured to draw fire and then rush in while the defenders had empty guns. However, there was no point in entertaining regrets.

The enemy began to spread out then and he saw that they were going to roll forward in a long thin line, probably with the idea of wrapping their attack right around the wagon fort. They were still walking their horses and Starke looked away long enough to see what was happening on the river bed. The bogged wagon seemed to be on harder ground now, but the men around it were cut off from their companions on the ridge. Diego seemed to be making some sort of defensive arrangements, but Starke didn't take time to see what they were. Diego would hold up his end of the deal; just now the important thing was to stop this impending charge.

He flashed a glance at the far shore, half expecting to see some of Pedro's men moving across the sands, but there was no movement there. He didn't know what to make of it, but again this was something he couldn't give attention to at the moment. A shout from the distant horsemen had indicated the beginning of the assault.

CHAPTER
THIRTEEN

It was hot beneath the wagon where Starke had taken up his position. The sun was now well up in the sky and Starke found himself guessing at the time. It came as something of a surprise to realize that it was close to noon. At this moment the train should have been far into the hills where the Imperials refused to go. Instead, it was tied in a knot on a scorching hilltop, getting ready to fight off an overpowering enemy.

He knew an instant of anger that Ritchie had been deceived by that fake officer, then tossed everything else aside to concentrate on the task at hand. Twice he called to his men, urging everyone to wait for the proper moment. Then he took careful aim at the man who seemed to be giving orders to the attackers.

His shot made the rider falter, but it was likewise the signal for the real rush, just as he had suspected. Evidently the enemy had gambled that the first shot would be followed by others, so that they could rush in upon defenders struggling to reload. Starke could almost see the indecision grip the oncoming riders when no other shots echoed his own. Still they came on, however, and he raised his head to shout his order. "Pick your targets. Make every shot count. Fire!"

A dozen muskets, carbines, rifles, and other assorted firearms blazed from beneath the wagons. Starke saw two horses go down and three or four men topple from their saddles. Then the remaining attackers swept in, only to be met by a peppering fire from dragoon pistols and Colt revolvers. Horses crashed into the wagons as their riders tried to get at the men who refused to come out and make targets of themselves. The Texans and Imperials were firing now but with little effect, the resulting din sending unpicketed mules into a wild stampede across the top of the ridge. Starke knew what was happening behind him, but there was nothing he could do about it.

He emptied his .44 as rapidly as he could pick targets, content to know that almost every bullet did some sort of damage. By that time the charge had broken and the frustrated enemy pulled back in dismay. The lesson had been costly but quick. They had learned that a man on horseback doesn't have much luck against a cool defender under a freight wagon.

An Imperial officer was howling commands in Spanish, trying to get men dismounted for hand-to-hand fighting, but a bullet cut him down even as he tried to make the guerrilla leader understand what he wanted. Starke expected to see someone follow up the hint and he shouted a warning to his men. Then the tide of battle eddied in a new direction. A burst of firing came from the river and Starke looked around to see Diego leading a charge upon the enemy's flank. Four men running up from the damp sands of the Rio Grande didn't appear very formidable, but they served to rattle the already disgusted Texans. One man turned his horse to ride away and was quickly followed by a second and then a third. In thirty seconds the attack was broken, the survivors in full flight.

Only then did Starke look around to see how his men had fared. What he saw was better than he had dared to hope. Twenty feet to his left a man lay with his face buried in the sand, blood staining the ground in a manner that told its own story. He had been shot through the head. At two other points men were bandaging wounds or performing that service for others. By contrast, the ground beyond the wagons was littered with casualties.

"Rodriguez," Starke called, picking a man who did not seem to be injured. "Take a couple of others and see to those wounded out there. Do what you can, but make sure that their weapons are taken from them. Pick up any guns they've left behind."

Then he swung around to survey the river behind Diego and his jubilant flankers. The last wagon was now coming slowly up the grade to dry ground, but that was not the important point. At last there was a show of action from the opposite shore. Pedro and his men were galloping into sight around a knoll.

Their attitudes indicated a chase, and as the fact made itself known to Starke he saw two of them turn to fire at someone who was still out of sight behind the high ground. That meant close pursuit; Pedro wouldn't have his followers waste ammunition in long range gestures.

Starke counted them as they pounded out upon the river sands, nodding in quiet satisfaction when he tallied nine. Pedro had not yet lost a man. That was better than he had dared to hope.

Suddenly a succession of riders broke out into the open, riding hard on the trail of the fugitives. Again Starke felt he could understand the emotions of the enemy. They had been outsmarted by the wily Pedro, prevented from joining their comrades for the attack upon the wagon train. Now they were determined to take their revenge for the trick that had been played upon them, at the same time joining in the attack which they probably did not know had already failed.

"Get those prisoners in here, Rodriguez!" Starke shouted. "The rest of you get back to your defense posts. Don't fire until Pedro and his boys are through our lines. Then blast them with everything you've got. Make sure you've got every gun fully loaded!"

The grins around him were confident now. Even the green-horns had picked up some of the spirit of the outfit. They had defeated overpowering numbers of the dreaded *Tejanos*. They could do it again.

The last wagon was hustled into position and teams picketed more securely so that there would not be additional mules to round up later. That was a point to bother Starke even before the fight was won. Time was still an important factor because of the certainty that reinforcements could be expected for the enemy. The train had to be gotten under way again, even though it would mean a running fight. Rounding up the stampeded mules would mean an aggravating and dangerous delay.

The defense was more formidable now. Diego and his men formed a valiant anchor on the north side of the circle, ready to shift so as to meet the attack from any angle. Starke kept the original garrison in the old position, believing that the main part of any new attack would come from the same quarter.

By that time Pedro's retreat had taken him to the middle of the river bed, twenty-odd horsemen now in full pursuit across the wet sands. Evidently Pedro had led them astray as long as he could manage and was now running for cover even though this meant bringing the enemy down upon the wagons.

Somehow that didn't sound just right either, and as Starke considered the point, he saw what was happening. Pedro's fugitives began to spread out, no longer following the safe path of the ford. They cut corners and dodged perilously close to sinkholes, creating a great deal of confusion and permitting the enemy to gain upon them.

It was dangerous work, particularly when the guerrillas began to open fire more heavily, but Pedro kept his men at it, drawing the enemy into a headlong rush. Only when the gap between pursuer and pursued had closed to perilous dimensions did he shout an order and send his men scurrying for cover.

Starke understood the strategy as soon as he saw what the riders were doing and instantly he changed his orders. "All men with rifles follow me. The rest of you hold your positions and be ready to beat off any other attack from this side of the river. Hurry, you riflemen!"

When Pedro ordered a cessation of the confusion, Starke's men were lined along the river bank. Including Starke himself, there were eight of them, all veterans of border skirmishing and all excellent rifle shots. Pedro's men dashed for the Mexican shore, following the line of the safe ford, while behind them men began to find trouble. Two horses went down almost simultaneously as they struck quicksand, while four others jammed behind them as the hurrying pursuers became careless.

"Cut 'em down," Starke ordered grimly.

A patter of fire was the reply, snipers taking careful aim at the men who had fallen into the river trap. For a moment or two the entire force of guerrillas bunched around the bogged horses, and Pedro halted his retreat to have his men pour in a volley. Meanwhile, Starke's riflemen were laying down a steady barrage, almost every bullet finding its mark in a man or a horse. The work wasn't pretty, but it was effective — the kind of fighting which generally marked the border warfare.

Suddenly the Texans began to retreat, leaving men and horses where they were struggling. "Fire at the retreating men," Starke ordered. "We can take care of the others later."

There was time for only a round or two from each man as the Texans drew out of range, but the result was another pair of casualties. Starke ordered a cease-fire and took a deep breath for the first time in what seemed like hours. Actually, less than twenty minutes had elapsed since the opening of the first attack.

"Harness up!" he shouted. "Diego, send men to round up the runaway mules. Pass the word for Pedro's boys to pick up any wounded prisoners left behind. We may need hostages before we get clear."

He went on with other instructions for getting the train in motion again. It seemed almost unbelievable that they had lost but one man while inflicting such heavy casualties upon the enemy. However, such was the case. Five of the defenders had suffered wounds, but only one was disabled.

"We've changed the odds a bit," he told Diego with satisfaction. "Now if we can get moving again without too much delay, I think they'll hesitate to attack us even along the trail."

"But you expect other forces to come up?"

"Probably. The Imperials will have sent a message as to what they were planning to do and we know that Rose's outfit is strong enough to have plenty of other men coming to the scene. We'll be safe if we can make the hills."

Diego nodded soberly and moved away, taking over many of the chores that had become so important. Starke suddenly realized that no one in the outfit had eaten since the previous evening, so he passed the word for the camp cooks to take over. It would not mean very many minutes' additional delay, since the meal could be prepared while the wagons were being made ready for the trail. They would be on the move at about noon with the men fed and ready for the hard hours ahead.

His calculations proved sound. The noonday heat was full upon the Rio Grande country when the reluctant Mexicans abandoned all thought of a siesta and shoved out toward the southwest, aiming for the blue hills which meant safety. Several of the wagons carried extra burdens of wounded prisoners, while Starke's wounded traveled in a different vehicle. Four men were unfit for service and the little cavalcade now traveled with but a tiny guard flung out on its flanks. Four of Pedro's scouts had been pressed into service as wagon drivers.

An hour of hot dusty travel brought the hill country appreciably closer, and still there had been no signs of pursuit. Twice the scouts had reported tiny dust clouds on the back trail, but on neither occasion did the cloud come closer or prove to be an enemy.

For Starke the minutes of respite brought a certain confusion of thought. He kept wondering about the man who had called himself Major Weldon. The fellow had certainly had a great deal of information, yet he had clearly missed a number of points. If there had been a traitor within the American camp, how had it happened that the information had been so lacking? Why was it that the enemy had not spotted Ritchie's column until so late in its march?

One uncomfortable thought kept coming back to annoy him. Suppose Major Weldon had been the real thing? Pedro could have been wrong in his identification. The Mexican might even have lied deliberately in order to get the wagon train moving again. In some ways Weldon's ignorance might actually have been the result of a real situation. An officer sent out hurriedly would not have been any better informed, yet he would have known which column to overtake. Starke didn't dare consider the consequence of the error if it actually was one.

Nor did he have time for such consideration now. His immediate responsibility was to the little command he had led successfully through the skirmish. Night was coming on rapidly and the Serranias del Burro were encouragingly close. Another decision had to be made. Could he risk a night camp where a reinforced enemy might overtake and attack once more, or should he risk killing his tired stock in order to push on? Diego had already galloped ahead, hopeful of rounding up additional men, but Starke couldn't count on that assistance. Word of the *Ley Marcial* had frightened too many men into hiding in the deeper valleys.

At dusk he compromised by halting the train without unspanning the teams. A rest and some hot food would help morale if he decided to shove on. In the interval he was hopeful that he might get a bit of information from some of the wounded prisoners.

He found most of the men surly and uncommunicative, bitter at their ill fortune, but then he realized that one of the lesser casualties was blaming his former leaders rather than his own bad luck. Starke promptly had the fellow carried toward one of the cooking fires where a bit of food helped to loosen his tongue.

He was little more than a boy, evidently one of the youngsters who had been drawn in to fill the dwindling ranks of the Confederate army during the final months of the war. To him the surrender of a man named Lee in Virginia had meant nothing. His leaders had told him to continue harassing Yankees and he had followed orders. Now a hole in the leg made him wonder why he had been so stupid.

Starke listened silently and then moved away, signaling for Pedro to take over. Many times they had worked the same game on prisoners, letting several members of the company grill the victims until someone else, usually Starke himself, came along to relieve the threat. Generally the relieved prisoner would talk pretty freely to the man who had appeared as his friend.

This time it didn't take long. Pedro and two other battle-dirty *vaqueros* blustered at the unhappy youth for some five minutes and then Starke pretended to drive them away, cursing volubly in English.

"That's what comes of us Texans fightin' among ourselves," he confided to the prisoner. "We get tangled up with some tough characters. I reckon it's about time we got together and stopped bein' so stupid."

"Seems like," the boy agreed. "I reckon we been battin' our haids against a wall anyhow. I figured when we crossed over to this side o' the river we wouldn't have to fight the whole dam' Yankee army, but I didn't know it would git just as bad."

Starke smiled sympathetically. "Bad judgment on the part of your commander. He should have waited for the rest of his force before trying a frontal assault."

"Yuh mean them polecats what didn't come up soon enough from the other side o' the Rio Grande?"

"Partly. However, I mostly referred to the rest of Lily's outfit. I figured he'd throw at least a battalion at us."

The prisoner spat disgustedly. "He ain't got a battalion closer'n Laredo. Our crowd was at Del Rio when we got word that the Mex's would try to hold them wagons 'til we could git here. It looked like we had plenty o' men for the chore, but one way or another it was all we could muster."

Starke questioned him closely but could learn little more. It began to seem certain that the man who had called himself Major Weldon had indeed been an Imperial officer trying either to divert the wagons for easy capture or to delay them long enough for this Texas detachment to come up. The prisoner didn't know the facts; he was merely passing on camp gossip. He was sure, however, that no additional forces were in the vicinity unless they were Mexicans. The Texans had been fooled so completely that their guerrilla army had been well scattered by the time Ritchie's wagons were located.

After a while Starke left him, passing the word for his men to unspan the mules and prepare to get a night's rest. With no chance of a renewed attack, it seemed like good policy to recoup strength and wait for Diego to appear with men and orders. After that, the delivery of the wagons to the proper Juarez officers would be mere routine. So far as Fred Starke was concerned the job was done.

When morning brought no sign of new enemies, he began to make plans. This shipment was supposed to be the basic one, providing the supplies that would let Juarez recruit men to handle subsequent trains of munitions. That meant more similar chores for Fred

Starke. General Merritt had mentioned thirty thousand muskets on the way from Baton Rouge arsenal and it was known that other supplies had been started toward the border before diplomatic circles halted the flow of aid to Juarez. Probably those supplies would have to be smuggled over as General Sheridan worked to swell the ranks of Juarez supporters. That was in the cards no matter what the diplomats said.

Diego came in with a dozen ragged vaqueros just after the wagon train began to roll toward the hill country. He reported that the *Ley Marcial* was driving fugitives into the Juarez camps. They were desperate and ready for action. This wagon train would fan their enthusiasm into real revolt.

As they rode, Diego grew increasingly happy and voluble. The key victory had been won! Now the more timid backers of Juarez would find courage, not only because supplies had been delivered to their leader but because the enemy had suffered defeat in permitting those supplies to get through. Serranias Starke had brought precious help from the United States. Every Mexican knew that no power could stand against the combined might of the United States and Serranias Starke!

The only dark cloud in Diego's sky at the moment was his concern about future supplies. It was imperative that they continue to come in, especially firearms. If the men could be armed, Juarez would have every chance to make his revolution succeed without the active intervention of the United States.

164

For an hour Starke stayed with the train, discussing the situation with the Mexican; then he cut away, leaving Diego in command and requesting only good treatment for the wounded prisoners. He hit the back trail, riding with the old caution. He had accomplished his purpose. Now to see how much trouble he would have in getting back to San Antonio.

CHAPTER
FOURTEEN

With his responsibilities behind him Starke found his thoughts turning constantly to San Antonio. He wondered what sort of reception he would meet there. Ritchie would have made a formal report of the transfer of the wagons and the Weldon matter would have been threshed out completely and with plenty of red tape. Probably the gold braid boys would be outraged at the way he had held up an army unit — even if he had been right in naming Weldon a fraud.

The prospect didn't bother him too much, however. He was more interested in estimating the future of Juarez aid. What was the temper of the government now? What sort of supplies were coming through for smuggling? Or would the help become open, thus taking some of the responsibility from Fred Starke?

An entirely different interest kept intruding into these serious considerations, but he knew better than to let his thoughts wander in such a direction. When a man has to work his way through three hundred miles of hostile country he can't afford to ride along with his mind on a sunburned blonde.

He used plenty of caution as he headed back along the line the wagons had so recently covered. He expected that the Imperials would make some attempt to track the contraband, but to his surprise he saw no sign of such effort. The country was as bare of life as its parched condition deserved. Here and there a lean Chihuahua peered at him from behind a forlorn clump of mesquite, long pointed horns shaking slowly as the wild creature prepared for flight, but otherwise the land was dead. No man seemed interested in this wilderness of glare, heat, and dust. There was no sign that either the Imperials or the Texas irregulars had even tried to scout the retreating wagon train.

He still had the desolate land to himself when he reached the chain of hills where his men had fought their battle. It was an hour short of noon and the blinding heat had even driven the buzzards away from the dead horses and mules. He paused long enough to study the ford and the far side of the Rio Grande, then pushed on across the wet sands, reasonably certain that no one would be foolish enough to be guarding the passage at this time of day. He even stopped in midstream, digging a hole and waiting for it to fill with muddy water in order to move ahead with a full canteen and a horse that had some wetness in his belly. In this country a man didn't forget water if he expected to go on living.

In mid-afternoon he picked up the sign that told him of the Texans' retreat. One part of the guerrilla force had crossed into the United States at the regular ford, meeting the riders who had been fooled so badly by Pedro's rear guard. Then the combined force had moved away to the east. Starke grinned wolfishly at the thought of what they had probably said to each other when they met. Texans didn't like the idea of taking a licking from Mexicans — and this lot of Texans had taken a good one.

He followed their sign until it was clear that they were heading into Del Rio. Since it was not likely that any army unit still remained at that point, he didn't think it would be smart to appear there. Accordingly he kept on to the east, by-passing the town and aiming straight for San Antonio. By this time the extensive maneuvers should be over and Merritt's command would be back at the dreary business of policing camp, guarding supplies, and watching the construction of Fort Sam Houston.

He continued to exercise precaution as he moved through the brown country. Comanche raiders had become quite bold in recent months, and now there was the added danger of outlaw bands of discharged soldiers. Even without the organized threat from the guerrilla forces, this was not healthy country for the traveler. Once, the Texas Rangers had made a good start in civilizing the region, but now the Rangers were disbanded, victims of the sweeping changes brought about by the fall of the Rebel government. Federal cavalry patrols were trying to fill the gap, but Starke knew better than to depend on them.

Twice within two days he met such patrols and each time he failed to learn anything from them. A couple of bored lieutenants and two platoons of grumbling troopers were ready to do nothing except curse the vile land into which they had been thrust. Neither unit had been a part of the big maneuver out of San Antonio. Neither officer had heard anything from his headquarters in nearly two weeks. No one was particularly interested in Juarez, Maximilian, the Diplomatic Service, Mexico — or Lieutenant Fred Starke. After two weeks in the mesquite all they wanted was an end of their tours of duty.

Starke didn't argue. Men were likely to get that way in this country. The *coraje*, the Mexicans called it. If a man didn't go berserk and kill a few of his neighbors he did very well. Starke understood and shoved on into the east.

He picked up a third patrol only half a day out of San Antonio and was lucky enough to learn that the outfit was heading back to the post. They had no more information than the other two patrols, but he rode along with them, thus avoiding any risk of a clash with guerrilla patrols. He didn't suppose that the Rose-Lily outfit would expect him to return so promptly, but it was just as well not to take too much for granted. Their information facilities had been pretty good in the past and they might know more than he thought.

The sprawling encampments were still flung across the low ridges north of the city, but he quickly discovered some changes in organization. Picket lines were well manned and the sentries were alert. Evidently the command had taken official cognizance of the rebellious organizations in the area.

A Negro infantry company now camped at the spot where the Juarez wagons had been spanned out, and Starke wondered briefly what had become of Ritchie's detachment. Then he rode on toward Colonel Haney's quarters, finding things unchanged there. Haney was standing at the front of his tent in earnest conversation with two lanky men in somewhat scuffed civilian garb. He glanced up briefly as Starke dismounted, apparently not realizing who the visitor was. Then he caught himself up and looked again, an exclamation of surprise coming from his thin lips.

"How did you get back so soon, Starke?" he demanded. "We didn't look for you for at least another week."

Starke shrugged. "Job was done. I suppose there's more to do."

Haney nodded emphatically. "Just what we were discussing. That shipment of muskets from Baton Rouge came into Corpus Christi last week and we're trying to decide how they should be handled. You're just in time to give us our answer. Can we transfer them along the coast, or do we have to run 'em back into the hills?"

Starke realized that the two citizens in mufti were studying him with frank interest. Evidently they were agents of Army undercover information, but Haney didn't introduce either of them. In their business it was safer to be anonymous.

"Still planning to help Juarez under cover?" Starke asked.

"No change on that score. If anything we're being a little more open, but officially we don't have anything to do with Mexican politics."

It occurred to Starke that Haney's interest in the new problem and his lack of concern over the past one answered one of the old questions. If the Weldon matter had been a mistake, Haney wouldn't be putting his new puzzle up to the man who had fumbled the first one.

"Get the stuff here first, sir," Starke suggested. "Juarez is recruiting fast and he needs the guns, but he can't control that country near the gulf. Not yet, at least. He can send a decent force to meet any train we send them now, but we'll have to move the stuff into the hill country to give him a fair chance. At least for the next month or so, our shipments will have to be handled much like the first one."

Haney didn't question his judgment. He turned to the others and nodded shortly. "There's our answer, gentlemen. Lieutenant Starke knows the situation better than anyone else. Have those guns brought to San Antonio at once."

Starke liked the sound of that. Evidently he hadn't come back to any red-tape trouble.

The two civilians departed promptly and Haney led the way into his tent. "Let's hear all about it," he invited with a smile. "I've heard the story in detail from Captain Ritchie's report and I'm all the more curious to get an informal version of it."

It took most of the afternoon, but eventually Starke managed to get his story told and to get his questions answered. Ritchie had returned to camp with four prisoners under close arrest, the masquerade having been dropped by them long before reaching San Antonio. Somewhere along the line of march Sergeant

McCall had worked on the two former Confederates who had posed as orderlies for the false officers. Both men knew that they had violated the surrender terms by crossing into Mexico and enlisting in the mercenary army of Maximilian. Consequently, they wanted to make the best deal possible for themselves and they talked freely in exchange for a promise of easy treatment. After that the other pair had broken down. The man who called himself Major Weldon was actually a Major Schwartz and the younger fellow was his orderly.

They had acted as spies for the Maximilian forces several times before and had used their captured papers without having them questioned. Since they had been handy at the time when it became important to delay or divert Ritchie's column, they had played their game on him, intending either to turn the wagons toward the border or to delay them while the Texans were bringing up their scattered forces.

"Ritchie made his report with a wealth of detail," Haney said with frank amusement. "He protested your improper threat against his camp, but he gave you full credit for seeing through the imposture. He couldn't seem to make up his mind whether to be outraged or embarrassed."

Starke grinned. He felt a little sorry for Captain Ritchie, but he still hadn't forgotten that Ritchie had put him in a bad hole. "I hope Sergeant McCall has been cited for his part in the show," he commented. "Not only did he get the confession you just told me about, but he carried a good load when things were

172

touch and go in Ritchie's camp. I depended on McCall to see that we didn't have any unfortunate clash and he came through with flying colors."

Colonel Haney's grin was almost a replica of Starke's. "I've already done something about that," he said quietly. "With the Juarez wagons out of the way, we sent Ritchie's boys back to being part of the Headquarters Company again, but I had McCall detached for special assignment to me. If you need him he'll be around."

"What happened to Major Weldon — or whatever his name was?"

Haney winked. "We're keeping him handy. Suppose a fellow of about your size happens to get picked up behind the Maximilian lines. We might need swapping material — or we might need an answer if somebody starts to get nasty about having one of our officers on the wrong side of the line. It could turn out to be real convenient to have our friend on tap."

"Fair enough. Anything else I ought to know?"

"Probably not. I've made a discreet contact with your friend Diego's headquarters in the Mexican section, the cantina you told me about. One of my men has become a regular customer there and we're getting along famously. From that source I hear that Rose and Lily are still moving around, but I don't hear of anything that sounds like immediate plans for action."

"They'll come up with something," Starke growled. "There's too much chance of loot in the situation for bandits like Miles Lily to stay quiet."

"I suppose so. For the moment I suppose they're licking their wounds and wondering what happened to them. Within a few days maybe I'll get a report about it."

"They'll be sore, all right," Starke agreed, his eyes narrowing as he thought about it. "And they'll be more careful next time. We won't fool them so easily and we won't catch them with their force dissipated into small units. Thirty thousand muskets would be quite a haul for a bandit crowd who could offer them for sale to the Mex faction that would make the best offer. My guess is that the Maximilian forces will be out to intercept the guns, and if they can't catch them first they'll be willing to pay plenty to keep them out of the hands of revolutionists. Rose and Lily are counting on this game being a double prospect, I'm sure."

"That's the way I've been figuring it," Haney said, his tone calm but grim. "That's why I'm dropping it squarely in your lap. My advice is that the State Department has no immediate plans for withdrawing the neutrality order, so you're still the man for the job. Get those guns smuggled across to Juarez any way you can make it."

Starke nodded, his squint a trifle more pronounced. "I've got an idea that this time we don't wait for them to hit us first. Let me sleep on it and I'll talk it over with you some more in the morning."

It was some time before he could get around to the problem. He had to set down the account of the fight in the hills, not as a report, but as a personal explanation to General Merritt. Undoubtedly the account, along

174

with Ritchie's earlier narrative, would get to General Sheridan, but there would be no permanent record kept. As a confidential matter that was beyond the strict interpretation of orders it could go no further. Starke reflected that he always seemed to draw this kind of duty. Promotions rarely went with accomplishments that had to be kept secret.

Still, he had come up with something of a plan when morning arrived. He took it to Haney immediately after breakfast and secured a promise of full cooperation. "There are two chores that need doing right away," he said at the outset. "One is to get those muskets up here from Corpus Christi and the other is to locate guerrilla headquarters."

"That latter point has been worrying me," Colonel Haney admitted. "We know that most of the outlaw riders are men who stay at home most of the time and pretend to be friendly citizens. They ride out secretly when called into action. However, there must be a hard core of permanent troops at some strategic point. They certainly have supplies and they probably have guns and ammunition which were held out at the surrender. Our patrols have been advised to keep an open eye for such a spot, but we've had no report of anything suspicious being found."

"I've got an idea on the subject," Starke told him. "When Miles Lily was operating around here early in the war he roamed the country between the Rio Grande and the Nueces. Later, when the Confederate authorities named him an outlaw, he went north into the hill country around San Marcos or a little to the west of that. I'd guess that his old hangout is now headquarters for his bandit army. I can't decide whether I should take a patrol into those hills or whether I should ride to meet the gun shipment coming up from Christi. It's just possible that our friends might try to hijack this shipment before it even reaches this point. It would certainly be one way of getting the jump on us."

"I'll help you on that decision," Colonel Haney said promptly. "We have plenty of men who can be detailed to convoy that shipment of muskets from the gulf. We'll have a regiment guard the wagons if you think it's necessary, but we don't have anybody around here who knows this Texas country as you do. You're the man to make the scout into the hill country, or wherever you think these outlaws might be basing their operations. One way to break them up good would be to strike hard at their organization and their leaders."

"I suppose you're right," Starke agreed. "I'd like nothing better. So far as Miles Lily is concerned, I've got a score to settle."

"Then consider that your next assignment. Let me know in the morning what sort of force you want to take. It'll be your party this time. You'll have full command and you'll be able to pick your own men."

Starke simply nodded his agreement. Several ironic comments came into his mind, but there was no point in expressing them for Haney's benefit. Haney wasn't to blame for the situation.

CHAPTER
FIFTEEN

When Starke opened his eyes next morning he was conscious chiefly of a vast annoyance at himself. Most of the night he had rolled on his cot, thinking contradictory thoughts. He had been as excited over the prospect of a formal independent command as though he were the newest shavetail. For the first time in three years he had the opportunity to go out decently in proper uniform at the head of regular troops. Half of the night he had spent in savoring the idea, while the other half had been used in realizing that such a surrender to professional vanity would be a great mistake. Miles Lily's hangout wouldn't be located by any such patrol.

Now wide awake and swinging long legs from the cot, Starke knew that he had ruined his night's sleep for nothing. It would take a brigade to search the hill country — or it could be done Indian fashion by a man or two with the skill and patience to wait and watch. All of that business about leading a command into the hills was sheer nonsense, too ridiculous for a man like Fred Starke to consider even in his sleep.

He groped for his boots and shook them out carefully. Even though he was in camp old habits held good. It wasn't much fun to push a foot into a boot that was already occupied by a centipede or a lizard. Along the border a man picked up those habits or suffered the consequences.

He was still angry at his own nocturnal foolishness as he began to lay plans for the project in mind. When he joined Colonel Haney at breakfast, he had a program that he could outline briefly but clearly.

"I'll want to slip out of camp tonight, accompanied only by Sergeant McCall, both of us in civilian garb. We should leave late enough to be inconspicuous, but early enough so that a night's ride will put us into the hill country by daylight. Then we'll hole up and play a waiting game. I feel sure it's the only chance we'll have."

"You're taking quite a risk, aren't you?"

Starke shrugged. "I've been taking risks ever since I started on this crazy series of jobs. This one won't be any more risky than the others. I know that hill country thoroughly and I'll be safer there than I was in camp here the last time I was around. Maybe safer than I'm going to be this time when the enemy finds out that I'm here."

"And you think you will have a chance to learn something?"

"I hope so. A couple of men with patience can learn more in the hills than a regiment could."

"How much patience? How long do you expect to be gone?"

"Maybe I'll get lucky. It could work out in a few days. One way or another I've got at least two weeks.

178

Those muskets won't be here from Christi before that. With a few bits of luck I might be able to make the further shipment a lot easier. Cleaning out enemy headquarters would sure put a crimp in their plans for any attacks on wagon trains."

"It's your choice," Haney told him. "You do it any way you want to. Just tell me what help you need at this end."

"Passes for both of us. Civilian clothing for McCall that will look as ragged as what I've been wearing. Two good horses with saddles and equipment that won't smack of the U.S. Army. Hard rations for two weeks. If you'll take care of that, I'll do the rest." He hesitated a moment before adding, "And maybe it'll be a good idea to have two or three good companies of cavalry on call for a quick dash into the hills. If we should get into a spot where swift action is needed, I wouldn't want to wait for marching orders to go through regular channels."

Haney chuckled dryly. "Your horror of red tape is exceeded only by my own. I'll take it up with General Merritt and have two crack outfits standing by at all times, subject to my orders. Then no one else will know what it means. They'll be on the trail within an hour from the time we get any word from you."

"Good. And keep it a secret all along the line, please. If the enemy gets word that I'm out there looking they'll probably send out some pretty good hill men to look for me."

"As of now there are just two of us in the secret. Sergeant McCall and General Merritt will make four. So far as I am concerned, that will be the end of it."

"Good. I'll see you later today and make arrangements to get the horses and equipment. Meanwhile, I'd prefer not to be seen doing anything that looks like preparatory work."

After breakfast Starke spent a half hour in close conversation with the lanky McCall, hearing a more private account of the Weldon affair and passing on his orders for the trip into the hills. McCall's questions indicated that he understood the nature of the task he was undertaking. Then Starke moved away again. He didn't want to remain with McCall long enough to attract notice. When the two of them turned up missing on the morrow he didn't want people jumping to conclusions. Even in the more closely guarded camp there would still be enemy agents.

The next move was quite different. His uniform was still in Colonel Haney's baggage, so he pulled it out and set an orderly to work sponging and pressing it. Meanwhile he secured the services of a company barber, getting a shave, haircut, and bath for the first time in over a month. A little after noon mess he checked his appearance with care and rode away from Haney's quarters, more than a little self-conscious. It seemed to him that every man in the regimental areas he skirted must know that here was a fellow cleaned up within an inch of his life because he had foolish notions about seeing a girl.

He had considered several direct methods of learning the whereabouts of Susan Mallory, but in each case he discarded the idea. Now he had some sort of vague thought that he could call on Major Mallory and find some pretext for inquiring about the supply officer's daughter. It didn't sound like a very smart idea even when he decided upon it.

Supply was still operating at the same old spot, the heavy traffic in freight wagons hinting that this was still the place for enemy spies to move in and out of camp. Starke halted for a moment to watch the flow of materials, wondering how many of the grimy teamsters within view were actually in the service of Lily and Rose.

Then he saw a white horse working its way through the wagon traffic and he forgot everything else. Luck had smiled upon him. Apparently Sue Mallory had been speaking to her father and was now on her way back to her own quarters or to some other spot. Suddenly Starke didn't seem to have any problems at all. Then he had them again. What was he going to say to her? How would he explain this obvious attempt to see her again? Nothing in their past relations had provided any excuse for a direct approach.

She saw him then and made it very easy, as somehow he had known she would. Lifting a hand in gay salute, she called, "Welcome home, Serranias Starke! I hear you've been swashbuckling again."

He swung his mount to ride beside her, conscious of the knowing stares that the teamsters were aiming at him. "Thanks for the welcome," he replied, matching her smile, "but what about that swashbuckling business? I didn't know I'd been accused of anything like that."

"You should hear Ned Ritchie." She laughed. "To him any man is a swashbuckler if he departs even slightly from regulations. Certainly the term would apply to a junior officer who had the nerve to invade a camp commanded by his superiors — and get away with it." She tried to sound severe, but the light in her eyes betrayed her. Starke had a feeling that she had been getting a lot of fun out of Captain Ritchie's indignation.

"My kind of duty doesn't give me much choice," he said quietly. "I have to do a lot of things which I wouldn't be able to do if I were on a regular detail."

"It certainly must be more interesting that way," she suggested.

"And sometimes more dangerous. But let's not talk about it. What do you have to report as our most efficient undercover agent?"

She turned her head to meet his eyes directly. "Do I understand that you sought me out only to get an intelligence report? I'm scarcely flattered."

"I'm shy," he confided solemnly. "I had to have some kind of excuse."

"I wouldn't have believed it," she scoffed. "Serranias Starke is not the man to need excuses."

He decided that he had been on the defensive long enough. "You're a fine one to make cutting remarks about my character! I seem to remember that you are the young lady who defied regulations to go riding across the river. You are also the girl who shocked everybody by helping that crazy Starke annoy some very dangerous characters at a dance. I think maybe you are something of a swashbuckler in your own right."

"Now I'm really flattered!" she exclaimed. "I was afraid you wouldn't notice."

"How could I help it? You don't have to be a swashbuckler to have every man within half a mile looking at you. Being a swashbuckler just makes you interesting, as well as pleasant to look at."

"Careful, Starke," she mocked, her voice dropping a little. "You are sounding remarkably like a ballroom swashbuckler now."

"Shame on me! That's what a shave and a haircut will do to a man who isn't accustomed to the luxury. Would it relieve some of the disgrace if I assured you I meant it sincerely?"

She did not reply for some minutes. They rode along at the edge of a regimental area, watching idly as recruits drilled in the glaring sun. Finally she managed to find her voice. "I'd like to believe you," she said simply.

Now Starke remained silent, not quite sure that he was hearing right. What she had said and the way she had said it told him that his hopes had not been too high. Finally he asked, "Is there anything I can do to make my remarks more believable?"

She shook her head, avoiding his eyes. "I don't know. I'm afraid I'm a little confused just now. When you were in camp before, you said little to me except to discuss the matter of Rose and my father. Now you make pretty speeches."

"At your request," he reminded her. "You didn't seem to be content with your role as undercover agent."

"My error," she snapped, all of the cordiality going out of her tone. "I'm sorry if I seemed to be asking for gallantry."

"Now wait a minute. I didn't mean it that way. I offered a compliment because I wanted to, because I felt that way about it. I've been doing a lot of thinking since that night when you played such a smart game at that dance. The more I thought, the more I felt certain that I intended to see more of you. If Captain Ritchie is the man, tell me so and I'll get out of the way. If he isn't, then I'm declaring myself a candidate."

Her voice was still crisp as she replied, but a lot of the ice had gone out of it. "A fair and open statement, sir. I accept it for what it appears to be worth. In exchange I offer the information that my father has made it quite clear that he expects me to marry Captain Ritchie. On my own account, I must say that sometimes the idea seems to have merit and at other times I'm not so sure."

He chuckled at the businesslike tone she had adopted. There was some of the old whimsy in it despite her basic seriousness and he felt that her moment of irritation was over. "Thank you," he said politely. "It is good to have a fair statement of the facts. Now I can feel free to promote the interests of Fred Starke."

"You have permission to do so," she agreed, still solemn. "I must tell you, however, that I have my misgivings about you. Perhaps they are really

184

misgivings about myself. I'm a little afraid that I'm too much aware of your reputation. As a swashbuckler, you know. I was quite thrilled to play a part with you at that dance. I can look back with pleasure on the way you saved me from those thugs across the river. Maybe I'm confusing Starke the man with Starke the swashbuckler. I want to know for sure before I commit myself."

"Holy Smoke!" he gasped. "You make me sound like something out of Sir Walter Scott. Do you mean that I'm supposed to calm down and be a little gentleman for a while so that you can make up your mind whether I'm still acceptable that way?"

"Something like that," she admitted. "You're making me sound pretty silly, but I'm really serious."

They rode in silence for several minutes after that. Finally Starke spoke. "Maybe you're thinking straight," he conceded. "I'm pretty mixed up myself. I'm just sure that I propose to marry you if you'll have me. I'll not even object to going on probation, but I'll have to warn you that I can't start being a gentleman just yet. In fact, I won't be around where you can watch my antics for some time."

"More smuggling?" she asked.

"Call it more swashbuckling," he grinned. "After that . . ."

They let it go at that and proceeded to spend a pleasant two hours, idly touring the camps and paying little attention to anyone except themselves. Sue asked no further questions about Starke's next assignment and he liked her more for it. She seemed to understand such things without having them spelled out for her, just as she had grasped the situation that night at the dance.

Twice Starke realized that passing teamsters were watching him and once Sue made a half-worried joke about the number of reports that would be going into guerrilla headquarters about the present whereabouts of Fred Starke. He passed it off without saying very much on the subject, not wanting to tell her that he was glad to have this afternoon's activities reported. It simply wouldn't be good judgment to tell a woman that her company was useful because it would give an enemy a wrong impression about future plans.

All in all, it was a pretty good afternoon and Starke went back to Colonel Haney's quarters with the feeling that a tide had turned. He had gotten the definite impression that Sue Mallory liked him a great deal, enough to be pretty frank about the test she wanted to make of her own true feelings. At the same time, he had been seen by several men who would pass the word to Robert Rose. A shaven and shorn Starke squiring a girl through the camp would not be expected to move out on a dangerous mission within the next few hours.

He had his supper with Haney, the time serving to let them exchange information. Starke outlined the plans for scouting the hill country and Haney told him where he would find his horses and equipment. After that there was nothing to do but to let the camp quiet down.

He slipped into his battered trail garb twenty minutes before taps and strolled across to where two saddled horses stood waiting. There was no guard with

186

them, but a rider came out of the shadows at once. His quiet greeting identified him as Colonel Haney.

"I'll get you clear of the camp," he announced. "The pickets are being hounded with strict orders just now and they might stir up a fuss. I'll go along myself so as not to let somebody else in on the secret."

"Thanks," Starke said simply. He purposely omitted the sir in grateful response to Haney's own dropping of formality for the occasion.

There was no trouble in getting out of the encampment. Taps sounded as McCall joined them and they started. Everywhere men were scurrying to get out of sight before an officer could make his inspection round. The sentries were beginning to pace a little more grimly, as though conscious that as of this moment they were on their own. Twice Colonel Haney identified himself to zealous sentinels, but in each case he failed to refer to the shadowy figures who rode behind him. At no point did they see anyone else.

Well beyond the border of the camp the officer pulled up and reached out to grasp Starke's hand. "I think we slipped out without anyone knowing," he said. "You take it from here. Luck."

That was that. Ten minutes later Starke and McCall angled into the main trail from San Antonio to New Braunfels. The night was theirs alone.

CHAPTER
SIXTEEN

Daybreak found them some distance northwest of the trail they had followed during the night. They stopped long enough to build a fire and to have a quick meal of coffee, bacon, and biscuit. Then they stamped out the fire and rode on into the brush-covered hills.

An hour later Starke called a halt, dismounting and tying his horse to a cedar. "We'll take an hour's rest," he said. "Plenty of riding ahead of us, so we'd better not be too rough on the ponies."

McCall dropped to the ground stiff-legged, speaking his astonishment as he left his mount and turned to where Starke was already sprawled on the ground. "More hills and more trees than I've seen since I came to this crazy state," he growled. "Didn't know you had anything down here but dust and mesquite."

Starke grinned. "We're just in the edge of the hill country," he explained. "Mostly rolling hills and a little decent timber. Mostly brush though." He rolled over until he was close to a patch of bare red clay where the rains had washed the slope. Using a stick, he drew a rough diamond on the smooth clay surface.

"You'd better know what we're about. The bottom point of the diamond is San Antonio. Top is

Fredericksburg, maybe sixty miles north. Over here to the east is New Braunfels. That west side is not important and it's not even sketched in good. The country's mostly the kind we're interested in though. Starting over here at New Braunfels, we'll draw a line right across the middle of the diamond, and that is the southern edge of the hill country. It goes north a good ways, but we're not likely to find Lily's hangout up that way. If I figure him right, he'll try to take advantage of the cover of the hills but stay as close to the border as he can make it. That's his field of operation, so he'll want his supply base as convenient as possible."

"Makes sense," McCall agreed. "Then we got to search along this line across here?"

"Something like that, only not so easy. The whole country's a tangle of brush and broken arroyos. It'll be tough to scout — and that's the very reason why I expect to find Lily's outfit holed up in it somewhere."

"Are we lookin' for a camp or for trails?"

"Either. I'd rather find tracks and follow them in. Blundering into a guarded area is awkward. I think our best bet is to hunt for the spots where his men have left the main trails going to or from the hideout."

"You mean there's more'n one way for 'em to head into this country?"

"At least three trails that could be called roads. We rode one of 'em most of last night. That was the road to New Braunfels. There's another that winds up along the left side of our diamond only a little more toward the middle. That's the one to Fredericksburg. Then there's a thinner trail about halfway between them. All three come from San Antone."

McCall nodded. "Then I reckon the Rebs are usin' all three so as not to show too much traffic on any of 'em."

"Likely. We'll have to scout all three. My guess is that this middle one is the best bet, so that's why we angled across from the New Braunfels road. When we move ahead I'll scout the ground for signs of any travel and you keep on the watch to prevent our blundering into trouble."

They found the plan a good one and by noon they had scouted well to the north, always keeping a little to the east of the rough trail which ran north between the other two main roads. At about one o'clock Starke called a halt at a spot where a clear stream ran through a break in the hills. The country was pleasant now, a little more rugged of terrain but with less brush.

"Looks more like Maryland than Texas," McCall observed. "In my book that's an improvement."

Starke laughed. "All in the point of view. I'd say that Maryland looks like this part of Texas."

They spent another lazy hour, aware that they had now put better than fourteen hours of riding behind them. The horses seemed able to stand it, however, and in midafternoon they pushed on through the hills, following the brook now. Less than a mile beyond their resting spot they cut the trail of perhaps a dozen horsemen who had recently ridden across the brook from east to west.

"This could be it," Starke said quietly. "If the hideout is near New Braunfels, this could be the tracks of a party riding out to hit one of the other roads south. If the place is farther to the west, this trail could have been made by men coming out from San Antone by way of the New Braunfels road."

He swung his mount toward the west and McCall asked, "Any reason for following the sign this way?"

"A couple of reasons. In the first place, I don't think Miles Lily would hole up close to New Braunfels. The folks over there are largely Germans and were Unionists during the war. Lily fought 'em and murdered 'em. They hate him for good reason and I don't believe he'd risk so much as to establish his main headquarters where some of them might stumble on him."

McCall looked up curiously at the changed tone of Starke's voice. He knew enough about the other man's record to recognize the undercurrent of emotion behind this reference to the New Braunfels Germans. Apparently the Germans weren't the only ones who held their hatred against Lily.

When Starke lapsed into a dour silence, McCall waited a few minutes before asking, "What was the other reason, sir? You said you had a couple."

Starke laughed shortly, as though trying to drive away a bad memory. "Easy enough. The trail up to Blanco is just west of us. We can check in a hurry to see whether these fellows were coming from a regular trail or going to one."

McCall didn't comment. He merely nodded his satisfaction. It was good to know that he was following a man who still continued to think straight even when angry emotions came upon him.

Five minutes later they cut the San Antonio-Blanco trail, crossing it only after Starke had dismounted and studied the sign from all directions. By that time both men were satisfied that the spot was not under observation, so they went on across, following the sign of a dozen riders who had done the same thing. Only when they had ridden another quarter of a mile did McCall sum up, as though trying to keep his own mind up to the pace Starke's was setting. "So these fellers we're trackin' came outa San Antonio by the New Braunfels road and cut across this way to head for the hideout, is that the idea?"

"That's the way I'm figuring it."

"Then the place oughta be close?"

"Maybe not. Lots of room between here and the Fredericksburg road."

They followed the sign until about an hour before dusk, always moving with due care but never seeing anyone. They were back into deep brush country again, country where the hills flattened out except for some ragged ravines and a few low bits of rocky outcroppings. McCall decided that this was not Maryland country any longer. More like New England at its worst.

They camped in a thicket where a little trickle of water ran down toward the flat brown country along the border. McCall was curious about that. There was water in the hill country, water that ran to the south, but there was no water down there toward the border.

"It dries up or goes underground," Starke told him. "It's another good reason why I figured Lily to have his main camp up in the hills. He can keep his stock in good condition for hard rides by grazing them up here. That border country's hell on horses."

That night they didn't risk a cooking fire, but at dawn there was enough land mist so that Starke thought a bit of smoke would not be noted. They had a quick fire, just enough to make coffee, and then the embers were quickly smothered before the smoke could become observable. Then they moved out once more, still following the sign they had picked up during the previous afternoon.

Within an hour they found more tracks. Men had ridden in both directions along a brushy path which appeared to be pretty well traveled. The sign they had been following angled into this beaten trail.

"Must be close in," Starke muttered. "They wouldn't permit such a trail to show at any distance out."

He motioned for McCall to pull back into thick cover and they held a short conference. Then they moved back again and picketed the horses. McCall was to remain with the animals while Starke scouted ahead on foot. With the outlaw camp so close, as he felt sure it must be, something like real Indian work was indicated.

Taking to the high ground that loomed on his right, he quickly realized where he was. He had roamed this region as a boy and the nature of the terrain came back to him at once. This was the spot where the stream took the wide bend around the rocky bluffs. At one spot it almost doubled back upon itself before finding an opening through the rocks. Meanwhile it managed to enclose a substantial wooded valley that was almost completely hidden behind the cliffs and the stream itself. Miles Lily must have seized upon this situation with great satisfaction. There was almost no chance of a search party stumbling upon his camp. The casual traveler would always detour to avoid the bluffs, probably never realizing that there was a valley behind them.

It made Starke wonder about the trail he had followed. That was the only vulnerable spot. Why was it that the trail wasn't guarded? At first he wondered whether he had stumbled into a trap, but then he decided that Lily's spies in San Antonio must have been sending reassuring reports. No one was making any effort to locate guerrilla headquarters; apparently the army didn't even suspect that such a spot existed.

I'll have to keep that in mind, Starke told himself. Pretty soon they'll learn that I'm missing and they'll guess that I might be doing exactly what I really am doing. Then they'll throw out pickets.

For quite some time he saw nothing out of the ordinary, then he spotted a thin trickle of smoke rising from the low ground to the west. He began to work his way to it, using plenty of care as he scrambled over the ledges and across the open places that scarred the ridge tops. It took him a good hour to reach the smoke, but eventually he lay on a flat rock where he could look down upon a broad clearing. There appeared to be a cluster of sheds or huts on the near side, but they were partly hidden by the bulge of the slope and he could see only the corners of what seemed like a regular line of them. There were large corrals, however, with many horses in them. Under tarpaulins he could see the stacks of boxes and bales, while beyond the corrals there was even a neat stack of baled hay. This guerrilla outfit was organized for quite a show.

An hour of further scouting told him little more than he had been able to see at first glance. No other vantage point gave him any better view of the clearing and he was not able to work into a position that would give him a chance to estimate the housing situation below. As yet he was not willing to risk scouting on the lower level. It would be time enough to get a line on manpower when plans were farther along.

Dusk was beginning to settle over the hill country when he slipped back into the little glade where he had left Sergeant McCall with the horses.

"Find anything?" McCall asked.

"It's there, all right," Starke told him with a quick nod. "I didn't find out as much as I want to know, but I saw horses enough for a couple of hundred men and supplies for a thousand. But I didn't see more than a handful of men. Maybe they're out of sight and maybe they're not in camp."

The lanky sergeant shrugged. "So what? If we've got the place located we've done our job. Nothing to do now but to report in and let headquarters order out enough of a force to squeeze the place good."

"Not quite," Starke told him, shaking his head. "I want to close the trap when I've got big game in it. This whole dirty business is a skin game run for the benefit of two men. Rose plays the respectable end of the deal, but Lily is the fellow who leads the men. If we get Lily we can break up the whole outfit. Without Lily, Rose is just another promoter with nothing to promote."

"But how are you going to know when Lily's there? And how will you make sure that he stays there until you get troops out?"

"I've been figuring on that point. Nothing sounds too good to me, but I'll outline the plan that I've worked out. If you don't find anything wrong with it we'll give it a try. Tomorrow morning you will head out of these hills and get back to Fort Sam Houston. I'll ride a way with you to make sure that you have a real knowledge of the backtrail. After I leave you at the Fredericksburg road I'll come back here and continue my scouting of that camp.

"Meanwhile you report back to Colonel Haney and tell him what we've found. Get a map and show him. We're maybe six-eight miles east of a little place called Boerno. You'll find it easy; there's a stream runs through there. I reckon it's the same stream that makes the big bend here. Tell Haney what we've got in mind about catching Lily and have him put his best men at the job of learning the enemy's movements. If possible, he should make sure that Miles Lily is not around San Antonio. If and when he gets any hint that the man is starting any kind of action, it'll be a pretty good hint that Lily will be here at his headquarters to direct activities. At that point Colonel Haney should arrange for a raid."

"General attack?" McCall asked.

"Not exactly. It'll have to be a surprise or our men will slip away into the brush before the troops can close in. I'd suggest that when the time comes for attack we should throw three full companies into the program. Have each one march out with light equipment, aiming in various directions. At an agreed time each company will cut back and take command of a road. When each road is blocked the attacking units can work up toward this point. You'll have to guide the one that comes by the Fredericksburg road, so be sure to remember your landmarks. They'll form the real attack; the others will serve to round up any stragglers."

McCall nodded. "I get that part all right, but what happens if the Colonel doesn't think it's smart to attack right away? Are you plannin' to stick around out here all that time?"

"Why not? I might get some ideas. Anyway I want to be handy to call the shots when the shooting starts."

They went over details until long after dark, McCall reciting his instructions until Starke felt certain that the man understood every part of the situation quite thoroughly. Then they rolled in their blankets for the night, content that there was nothing more to be done except to carry out plans.

At daybreak they were on the move, working out to the west and across the trail they had followed on the previous day. There had been only one change in the message McCall was to take back to Colonel Haney.

That was to the effect that if Starke should spot Miles Lily in the outlaw hideout he would ride for help at once. Against that possibility Haney would be asked to have troops ready for instant call.

They encountered no one and saw no new sign until they were almost out to the Fredericksburg road. Then they spotted the trail of four men who had apparently ridden out to the road. "Just as it first appeared," Starke muttered. "They fan out when they leave the hideout, taking various roads so that no one will see too many of them in any one place."

No one was in sight when they struck the road, so McCall jogged away at once, first making certain that he had his landmarks spotted. Starke watched his departure with some misgivings. The redhead could probably pass himself off as just another wandering ex-soldier if anyone stopped him, but it was still a big risk to take when so much depended on his getting through.

There was no point in worrying, though, and Starke headed back into the brush, intent on making certain that there were no other marked trails that he had missed. When he had spent the entire morning circling the rocky fortress, he felt certain that no substantial number of men used the place. It was a headquarters and a supply depot, not a troop center. That conclusion fitted with the idea that this entire guerrilla organization depended on keeping most of its personnel in the open posing as peaceful citizens.

Late in the afternoon, after he had found a safe hideaway for his horse, he ventured to stalk the clearing from the valley level, trying to make certain of his conclusions about the outlaw garrison. He quickly discovered that the shacks he had seen from above were few in number, apparently ammunition storage sheds for the most part. Only one cabin seemed to be set up for living quarters, the dozen or so men lounging in the valley having brush shelters for their camps.

He watched it all with due care, intent on memorizing details. The attack on this hideout might well solve most of the troubles on this side of the border, and he didn't propose to let anything go wrong because of faulty observation on his part. In fact, he was so busy concentrating on the scene in front of him that he neglected his rear. It was only when a twig snapped just to his left that he even considered the possibility that the outlaw crowd might have patrols out. Then it was too late. He turned to find himself looking into the muzzle of a Colt .44, which was all the more menacing because the man behind it was the bewhiskered gent who had been with Eli that afternoon at the edge of the Mexican quarter.

"Go ahe'd and try fer yer gun, Starke," the man urged. "Cap Lily might not like it if'n I was to gut-shoot yuh, but I'd like it fine. Jest gimme a good excuse!"

He grinned wolfishly, showing brown teeth with a number of gaps. Then he raised his voice to yell, "Git over here pronto, yuh polecats! Come lookit what I found."

CHAPTER
SEVENTEEN

Starke had found himself in a lot of tight places during his years on the border, but he couldn't recall one that disturbed him more. One moment of carelessness had brought disaster, not only to himself but to a lot of other people. In the split second of dismay he suddenly saw how big this thing had become. The outlaw ring was the nucleus of resistance to Federal authority. There would be no peace for southern Texas while Lily and his gang could stir up trouble. At the same time they would interfere with the problem of getting foreign troops out of Mexico. They were the firebrands who were keeping the entire border in a blaze of violence. In an unguarded moment Starke had thrown away the chance to strike a telling blow at this organization. Only incidentally he had spelled disaster for himself and his newly developed bright dreams.

The split second of understanding also brought the coolness of desperation. It was no time to be thinking about the extent of a disaster. A man had to keep trying, working to outguess the enemy. And this particular enemy was a clown. He was trying to be heavily humorous now, just as he had made drunken jokes when Eli was struggling with Sue Mallory. Maybe the man was as foolish as he sounded.

"Shoot to kill!" Starke shouted suddenly. "Gun him down and let's get out of here!"

Maybe it was clever acting on Starke's part. Maybe it was simply that the bearded man was the shallow comedian Starke had picked him to be. Maybe the fearsome reputation of Serranias Starke made the fellow expect to find a crew of hard-bitten Mexicans behind him. At any rate, he fell for the time-honored ruse, lunging to one side and shooting a swift glance behind him. The break was only momentary, but it was enough for Starke. He made his play as the bearded man jumped, drawing his .44 and slamming in a shot at the enemy's middle.

The bearded man's gun exploded almost in unison with Starke's, but the slug went wild and then the man was down, the gun dropping from his fingers as he rolled in pain. Starke leaped toward him, scooping up the fallen gun and continuing on into the deeper brush. Already he could hear the crash of bushes as other men ran toward the sound of the firing.

He had not gone fifty feet when he realized that he had made a mistake. He should have killed the bearded man to prevent his report, but it was too late now. Already he could hear the yells of pain changing to cries of something more articulate. Already the enemy knew that their camp had been scouted by their blood enemy.

Starke halted, partly because he didn't want to continue making noises that would betray him, and partly because he wanted to know what sort of pursuit to expect. A master at retreats, he had long since learned that the successful escape was not necessarily the swiftest. A fugitive often did well to remain close to his pursuers. Then he knew what they were doing and could prepare to cope with it.

He became a veritable Indian once more, quickly discovering that the enemy knew a few things about this business also. Instead of beating the bushes for him, they were organizing. Already men were running for their horses, preparing to throw a circle of guards around the area. They were not in any hurry to catch Serranias Starke; they just wanted to make sure that he didn't get out of the hill country.

Starke considered his own course with some care. It would take a good twenty minutes to reach his horse. By that time the men who had ridden away from the hideout would have passed the word on to the others who were probably posted for just such purposes. It seemed likely that he could still get out of the hills before any numerous patrols would get into operation, but there would be considerable risk of discovery. The enemy was alert now; they knew where to look for him.

Knowing the hill country as he did, he was pretty sure that they couldn't run him down in it any more successfully than a body of troops could comb it thoroughly enough to locate the outlaw headquarters. If the pursuit really grew hot he could still work around to the north and slip away. This was his own country and he didn't think anybody could catch him in it.

At the same time he realized that his presence in the brush might be turned to advantage. There would be a concentration of enemy force in an attempt to trap him, a concentration which might offer plenty of game for a sudden swoop by the Federal troops. Actually this had the making of a pretty fair trap — with Fred Starke as the bait. He could only hope that Haney's intelligence service would pick up the proper information so that the military authorities would know when to make their move. It could get pretty awkward if they waited too long.

At dusk he moved in on the clearing, really playing Comanche now. Twice sentries padded near him, but he avoided them without difficulty, presently reaching a spot where he could overhear fragments of conversation. It did not take long to learn that the enemy strategy was just what he had anticipated. They were not going to send men into the brush to play games with a fox like Serranias Starke. Instead, they had simply put out a general call for men and were arranging to have every road and back path guarded by sentries in pairs.

"We'll get him," a heavy voice predicted confidently. "Keep him bottled up long enough and he'll make a move. That's when we cut him down."

"Suppose he just lays low?"

The first speaker laughed. "Starke? Not him. He'll git itchy and figure he's got to make a move. That's the kind of a critter he is."

Starke decided to appreciate the compliment. It was interesting to know that the enemy credited him with a certain amount of energy. Interesting and at the same time valuable to know. If he wanted to fool them he had only to keep quiet.

He did that resolutely for two full days, never leaving the little ravine where he had first hidden his pony. At the end of that period he had gotten all of the rest he needed and was beginning to chafe at the lack of action. Maybe he was playing into the enemy's hands, but he decided that he would have to make a mild move. He had scouted their camp in safety before; no reason why he couldn't do it again.

Still, he waited until midafternoon of the third day before moving out into the brush afoot. Again he forced himself to play Indian, finally slipping in toward the clearing to take position near the line of sheds. More men were in the clearing than he had seen before and he decided that they were guard replacements. The cordon they were throwing about the southern edge of the hill country would require replacements, and the obvious place to base them was here.

The men seemed restless, expectant, and Starke moved in as close as he dared, trying to hear something that would explain it. They were gloating over something, he realized, but the only fragment of conversation which came to his ears left him puzzled.

"... when do yuh figger ... ?" It was part of what seemed to be a lengthy question.

The hard-bitten man who answered it spoke in a louder tone and Starke could hear quite plainly. "Mebbe another hour. They won't git the wagon through real fast, yuh know. But don't go gittin' anxious; it ain't goin' to be nothin' fer yuh to git excited about."

The pair of them moved away then and Starke settled down to wait. If something was due to happen in an hour, he intended to be on hand to see what it was.

Actually it was almost two hours before a hail announced someone coming in along the hidden trail. By that time the shadows were heavy across the little valley, and Starke wormed his way forward another risky yard in order to get a clearer view. Everywhere men had come out to watch, their attitudes showing that this was what the camp had been warned to expect. Starke guessed that it would be Lily and some of the other leaders coming to start a real search for their lurking enemy. That would be bad! Lily in the trap and nobody to get word to Colonel Haney.

As he condemned himself for getting into such a mess, he caught a glimpse of a little column of riders coming out of the brush. It was Miles Lily, all right, who led the way, a slightly heavier Lily than Starke remembered him to have been on that bloody day along the Nueces but unquestionably the same man. The beetling black brows and lantern jaw were unmistakable.

Then he ceased to stare at Lily. The fifth rider in the line was a woman, a blonde girl who held her head defiantly high in spite of the blindfold across her eyes and the thongs which fastened her wrists to the horn of the saddle. Even if he had not recognized the familiar riding costume he would have known that the prisoner was Sue Mallory.

For a moment anger almost made him do something foolish. His hand went to his gun and he started to pull his legs up under him. Then sense returned and he went down on his belly again, watching with eyes that never blinked, eyes which held only grim determination.

The phrase about the wagon made sense now. They had captured Sue, probably while she was out riding, and had smuggled her north in a wagon, placing her in a saddle only when they were clear of the open country. But why? What could these men hope to do by taking such a prisoner? The United States army couldn't take account of hostages, even if the hostage happened to be an officer's daughter. All in all, it seemed like a pretty foolish move on the part of Miles Lily and his gang. Until now they had been moving around almost as they pleased; now they were certain to have all kinds of military units hounding them to earth.

Then he realized that such was not necessarily the case. Maybe the military wouldn't know who had taken the girl. Maybe it would be blamed on Mexicans or almost anyone else. Then why had Lily seized her?

It took a real effort of will to remain quiet while two smirking hoodlums pulled the girl from the saddle, forgetting to free her hands and creating confusion when she remained fast to the saddle horn. Miles Lily bawled curses at them while the other men hooted in derision. Starke was reminded of the way Eli and his partner had acted; these men were taking a malicious

206

joy in heaping indignity upon a Yankee, even a helpless woman.

Through it all Sue made no effort to help herself or to strike back at the men who were handling her so roughly. At first Starke was afraid that she had been badly injured, then he caught the tilt of her head and realized that she was simply displaying her disdain for her captors. They would have liked to see her cringe, but she was ignoring them as completely as if none of this were happening.

Their uneasy milling hinted that they understood what she meant and were angered and baffled by it. Then Lily went to her and removed the blindfold, at which point several of the men slipped back into the deepening shadows. Starke wondered about that blindfold. They had prevented her seeing the trail into the hideout, but they were not trying to hide their faces from her. This in spite of the obvious fact that some of these men were playing the role of honest citizen on the outside. It didn't add up to anything very cheerful.

Lily made a little speech after he removed the dirty rag that had been tied around her eyes. Starke could not hear the words, but the gestures were eloquent. Lily was offering her the freedom of the camp — with the proper amount of mockery, of course — and reminding her that there were plenty of armed men to see that she did not slip away.

If Starke had not been so worried he would have enjoyed the girl's exhibition of courage. She turned away from Lily as if the man did not exist. Then she proceeded to inspect the camp, studying the ammunition shacks, the supply piles, the corrals, the hay piles — everything which the increasing gloom permitted. But she never seemed to notice any of the men who purposely put themselves in her way. When it was finally too dark for her to see anything very far from the cooking fires, she came back toward the corner of a corral and sat down there, still acting as if there wasn't a man within miles.

This was the moment when Starke most wished that he could slip her a word of encouragement. While she was walking, putting on her act, she would be keeping up her self-control. Now she was likely to let her emotions get the upper hand. He knew how it would be; for the past hour he had been forced to lie quiet while every nerve and muscle in him strained toward action, however wild and foolish.

The men had gathered for supper by that time and he noted that Lily was holding some kind of confab not too far from his hiding place. It was a dangerous thing to move just now, but he risked it, inching closer to the fire where a dozen men ate and talked. Soon he could hear part of the conversation and by the time he was within easy earshot he already knew what it all meant. Sue Mallory had been brought in for just one purpose, as bait for a trap that was to catch Serranias Starke.

The trap idea seemed to work two ways, Starke thought wryly. He had considered himself as bait for the purpose of getting Lily into reaching distance for the military, but instead Lily had used the trap in an entirely different manner.

208

"We'll keep her out in the open all the time," he heard Lily tell his men. "Where that damn Starke kin see her. He'll be awatchin' this camp from somewhere up on the rim, yuh kin bet, and sooner or later he'll see what's happened to the filly."

"Likely he knows already," another voice cut in. "Don't never figger he ain't a step ahead."

"No matter," Lily growled. "This time we got him where it hurts. We'll let him see her roamin' kinda loose around the camp, and unless I misfigger plenty he'll start itchin' to try some of his fancy tricks. That's when Mister Starke gits his come-uppance. We'll have pickets out all around, but nobody shows hisself. We let Starke in any time he wants to come — but then we cut him down. Fer keeps!"

He went on into detail as to how the guard would be mounted and Starke realized that the man was planning smartly. A line of sentinels could be passed, but a line of ambushers was another matter. Apparently the camp was to be guarded by at least a score of men at all times. No one was to show himself, but each one would be placed at a strategic spot. In addition, there were to be two men detailed to Sue Mallory. They would not interfere with her, but their job was to keep her constantly in sight. If Starke broke through in any kind of headlong dash they were to gun him down. If they failed they would at least alert the outer guards, whose job would be to keep him from getting back into cover. It sounded like a pretty deadly plan.

CHAPTER
EIGHTEEN

Starke watched for the better part of two hours, studying every move of his enemies, although mostly he found it hard to keep his eyes away from Sue. He decided finally that the girl was in no immediate physical danger. That might come later if her captors decided that they needed to make the bait a little more compelling, but tonight they were obviously just planning and preparing, clearly working on the assumption that the deadly game would have its opening moves on the morrow.

That was a clear hint, Starke thought. If the enemy expected to be hit tomorrow the obvious thing was to fool them and strike tonight. It sounded smart, but it would involve extra risks. In another day he would be able to learn something about guard assignments and other details of the trap. Maybe he would even be able to locate a weak spot at which he might strike. Tonight he would be blundering in the dark.

He considered the alternatives with due care while he watched the camp, finally coming up with the idea that an immediate attack would have advantages to offset the drawbacks. Already he knew where two of the outer pickets had taken up positions. Both of them had simply hunkered down under trees where they could watch the camp. He also knew that the guards were to be changed at midnight and again at four o'clock. A border raider ought to be able to make something of that.

Finally he slipped away, climbing the ledge with all possible stealth. The night had turned ominously quiet and he didn't want to make a sound that would warn the enemy of his presence. What he planned to do was entirely dependent upon surprise for its slim chance of success. A betraying sound now would ruin everything.

The starlight was bright enough to enable him to locate his pony without much difficulty and soon he was on his way again, leading the horse carefully through the brush. He did not believe that Lily had scouts in this part of the woods, but he still preferred slowness to extra risk.

It was well past midnight when he approached the hideout once more, this time circling southward in the direction of the hidden entrance. If his plan succeeded he wanted his horse where he could find it in a hurry, yet he didn't want to take the animal too close to the clearing. It occurred to him that the spot where McCall had waited for him would do quite well. It was handy but still far enough off the trail to keep the animal out of sight of any casual rider.

He was picketing the pony when something jammed hard into his back and a voice hissed, "Put up the hands! Quickly!"

Starke obeyed, his quick feeling of dismay being followed by one of a much more pleasant nature. He made his voice sound completely casual as he murmured, "Nobody but an educated Mex like Diego Menendez would say 'quickly' at a time like this. What's going on?"

He heard the Mexican utter a little gasp of surprise and then the pressure of the gun muzzle disappeared. "Starke! So it is you. In the darkness I could not tell."

"Naturally not. But don't waste time. How come you're holed up at such a spot as this?"

Diego chuckled. "I should claim special prescience, I suppose, but the fact is that I talked long with your Sergeant McCall. He told me of this spot, giving me the landmarks for finding it."

"But how did you happen across McCall?"

"Perhaps I should start from the beginning," Diego laughed shortly. "It is rather complicated. Juarez has heard of the shipment of muskets, so I am sent posthaste to San Antonio to find you and arrange for a quick delivery. I do not find you, but I find Sergeant McCall, who tells me of this place. He has just come from here and he takes me to your Colonel Haney who seems to understand much. I learn of your plan for trapping Captain Lily, but I think it might be well if I were to come out here ahead of time and see if perhaps I can be of assistance. I must get you out of this mess, you see, so that I can use you for my own purpose."

"Undoubtedly with some good adage from Cervantes as moral backing for such selfishness," Starke put in.

"Tonight I do not quote. Unless you like the bromide about Heaven helping those who help themselves. Not from Cervantes, of course. The thing you should know

212

is that I stumbled upon a nasty development as I made my way here. From a vantage point in the brush I saw some of our enemies transferring a prisoner from a wagon to horseback. I could not be certain, but it seemed to me that she was the lady who played that fine game with you while I passed a note to your Captain Ritchie. The captain's betrothed, I believe."

"That's the girl," Starke told him shortly. He preferred not to make any comments about that latter assumption. "She's held by Lily and his outfit as a sort of bait for enticing me into doing something foolish."

"And you have decided just what that foolishness will be?"

"In general. They're not expecting me to make any kind of a move just yet, so I had a notion that I might play the long shot about the time they change guards on the graveyard shift. They're over-cocky anyhow and most of 'em will be pretty sleepy about then."

"Sounds like a good bet. How do we get the girl's attention?"

"We?"

"Of course. Did I come into these disreputable hills just to watch you play hero?"

"Thanks. Nobody I'd rather have to side me, but you've got a job to do — and the odds are pretty long that we won't get away with it. We'll have anywhere from thirty to fifty pretty good brush men on our necks in no time at all."

"A fair handicap," Diego said calmly. "I believe it was Plutarch who records a conversation in which one soldier remarks that they are fallen among enemies. To

213

which his sturdier companion retorts, 'How are we fallen among them more than they among us?' We make the play. That is to our advantage."

Starke grinned in the darkness. When Diego started being literate he was dangerous. "Fair enough, *compadre*. You're in. I think I can use you. First, however, two questions."

"Ask, of course."

"You have a horse here?"

"Of a certainty."

"Good. Do you think there is any chance that the folks back at Sam Houston will know what happened to Miss Mallory?"

"That I do not know. I do know, though, that Lily has been under surveillance by agents of your Colonel Haney. When he rode out to this place today he most certainly was observed. In a short time the word will have gone back and the plan for trapping him will have been put in motion. With good fortune, there should be cavalrymen covering every approach to these hills by dawn."

"But they won't know to do anything except close in as planned?"

"Probably not."

"Then we won't wait. You and I will hope they are not too late to rescue us, because I've got a hunch we're goin' to get ourselves in one sweet hell of a mess."

They remained where they were for better than an hour, Starke sketching in the picture for Diego and outlining his scheme for getting Sue Mallory away. There was all the more reason for attempting a rescue now because it seemed certain that a full scale attack on the hideout was only hours away. Since the troopers who would assault the camp would not know of the girl's presence, she would be in danger of their bullets even if she escaped death at the hands of her captors. Of the two threats, Starke feared that the latter was more probable.

Half of a yellow moon was just climbing into the eastern sky when the two men left the spot by the brook, moving cautiously through the brush toward the outlaw camp. Starke guessed that it was three o'clock. That gave them an hour to get ready and to locate the pickets before the change of shift. After that they would have to make some pretty good guesses on timing if all were to work out properly. The plan was a ticklish one, but it was just crazy enough to work.

They kept together until Starke halted the advance, motioning for Diego to hold his position. Then he reconnoitered briefly and returned to report, "Same as it was. My two men are in the same places. Come on."

He led the way once more, presently halting at the far corner of the clearing near the supply piles. "Take your time," he advised. "Get close, but don't get caught. When they change guards, you can locate your men. Wait ten minutes after the guards change. I'll do the same. Then allow twenty minutes to get rid of the guards. That leaves us still a good half hour of safety margin before dawn. I'll wait for your move before I take the plunge."

"*Con Dios*," Diego said softly. Then Starke was working back the way he had come, skirting wide to avoid the picket line.

He reached his observation post just in time to see the stirring of a smouldering camp fire as someone started to rouse the relief guards. He could see the huddled bundle across by the nearer corral and knew that Sue rested there. He didn't know whether to think she had been able to sleep, but at least she was taking it easy. Which was a good thing; she might need a lot of energy before the next few hours passed.

If I get her out of camp, he added to himself, his thoughts grim. On the face of it the whole attempt seemed foolhardy. Here were some twoscore or more of hard-bitten outlaws who had laid a trap with just one thought in mind, to kill Fred Starke. Now Starke was proposing to step deliberately into the trap, proposing to do exactly what his enemies wanted him to do. It didn't make much sense, but he still proposed to give it a good strong try.

He watched the men around the fire as they swallowed coffee before taking over their posts. There seemed to be some sort of talk going the rounds, but presently an officer broke up the group and the various men headed for their positions. The pair who were watching Sue didn't bother to leave the fire, but the others fanned out in all directions and Starke counted them. Ten in all. Twelve men awake meant that some of them had done early guard duty also. The camp ought to be pretty sleepy now.

He could hear the muttered comments as the two men nearest to him were relieved; the new pickets settled down beneath trees and the pre-dawn blackness became silent once more. Starke waited until the men going off duty were rolled in their blankets, then he started to count, trying to make his ten-minute estimate match that of his comrade on the other side of the clearing. Ten minutes wasn't much time to allow for letting men get to sleep, but dawn would be just over the eastern horizon and too much delay could not be allowed.

When the allotted time was up he made his move boldly, standing up to approach the man who was closest to him on the north. He didn't try to make his move a quiet one and the man challenged quickly. Starke growled, "Come off it. Yuh're gittin' awful proddy jest because Lily wants yuh to play sojer. I come out here without no chawin' terbacker. Got any on yuh?"

He was trying to imitate the voice of the man he had heard taking over the next post and evidently the mimicry was good enough when it was done in a hoarse whisper. The guard grunted irritably and retorted, "Yuh don't never have nothin' of yer own, damn yuh! Well, come on and git it."

By that time Starke was within reaching distance. When he reached, however, he did so with a gun in his hand, slamming the weapon hard down on the head of the guerrilla picket. The man did not even grunt. He simply went loose all over and dropped to the ground.

Starke bent quickly, binding and gagging his man with belt and neckerchief before seizing the man's fallen weapon. "A little more time this way, but you ought to appreciate it," he told the unconscious outlaw. "The pair on the other side probably won't make out this well with that educated son of a gun to handle 'em."

Then he was moving back through the brush toward the picket who was next beyond his old listening post. Again he made shift to imitate the growling whisper of a man who was disobeying orders to leave his post in quest of tobacco. This time he almost met disaster.

"What're yuh doin' chawin' terbacker?" the other guard demanded. "I thought yuh only smoked the stuff in that stinkin' pipe yuh got."

Starke came up with the obvious answer in spite of his surprise at the reply. "Can't smoke now, yuh fool!"

By the time they had exchanged that many pleasantries he was close enough. Again he quieted his man without any show of resistance, again using the fellow's own belt to tie him up and his bandana to gag him. He had hit hard enough to be fairly sure neither man would wake up for some time, but it was just as well to play safe.

He tried to think back over the time he had taken and decided that he had not missed very far from using the twenty minutes allowed. Diego would be ready. With him there would have been no time lost in tying prisoners. For a man of such classic education he had a definitely ruthless streak.

218

The next move was the hardest of all. He simply walked out of the brush into the clearing, making no pretense of hiding and depending on the guards' taking him for one of their own number coming into camp for some reason or other. He started toward the fire but angled off almost at once as he saw a flicker of a match across the clearing. At any moment now the uproar would start and he wanted to be well on the inside when that happened. In the darkness he had to depend on their taking him for one of the gang.

Ten steps without an alarm. Ten more, the flicker of the match now a blaze that should draw a cry of alarm any minute. Not thirty feet ahead of him he could make out the dark figure of Sue Mallory on the ground. Her guards were still by the fire, neither of them having paid any attention to the man who was slouching across the camp.

"Fire!" The shout came from a picket at the far end. It was taken up by several others as the blaze mounted swiftly on the side of a stack of baled hay. A man came running out of the brush, but a gunshot cut him down in his tracks. Instantly there was a rattle of gunfire from that end of the camp and men began to run toward the scene of disturbance.

Starke turned to shout at the guards by the fire. "Get down there pronto!" he ordered, his tone so crisp that both men started to run without stopping to ask questions. They had no more than turned their backs when he was at Sue's side, rolling her free of her blankets with a heavy hand.

"Sue!" he snapped, his voice low but urgent. "Come up running. It won't take a minute for them to gather their wits about them. Hurry!"

The girl obeyed swiftly, uttering only a single gasp of surprise before springing to her feet. Starke shoved her in the direction of the woods. "Try to make the cover of the brush. Don't wait for me if the shootin' starts."

For several seconds they were unchallenged. The blazing hay and the continuing gunfire had evidently confused everyone. Men awakened abruptly from exhausted sleep were running toward the sights and sounds of trouble, adding to the uproar by shooting at anything that moved. Here and there a voice was raised in hoarse command, trying to stop the men from firing at each other and to get some sort of fire brigade organized. Diego had certainly done a thorough job of demoralizing the outlaw camp. One match and a couple of gunshots had turned the place into a noisy inferno.

Starke had time for a grim moment of enjoyment, then a voice challenged sharply. "Where are yuh goin' with that gal?"

Starke tried to carry on with the deception. Without turning his head he replied, "Got orders to put her in one o' the cabins. Got to git her away from the fightin'."

It didn't work. The other man came toward him with a rush. "Who gave any orders like that? Git back to . . ."

By that time Starke knew that he faced Miles Lily himself. Apparently Lily recognized Starke at the same time. At any rate he went for his gun.

Starke shoved Sue Mallory hard toward the woods and whirled to throw himself into a sideways lunge. He heard Lily's gun roar, but somewhat to his surprise he did not feel the impact of a bullet. Then his own .44 was bucking against his palm, almost without conscious effort on his part. He let the weapon belch out three of its deadly slugs, then hurried after Sue, not even waiting to see Lily hit the ground. At that distance he knew that he could not have missed.

Someone near the fire was getting control of the men now and shots began to rattle more venomously. Starke heard slugs whine over his head and knew that his sortie had been discovered. He turned to blast a pair of shots at his nearest pursuers and in the next instant was among the bushes, bent low and following the noise of the girl's flight. Several bullets crashed through the trees above his head; then the fusillade died away.

A couple of distant shots hinted that Diego was still working to create a diversion, but a glance back into the clearing told Starke that the enemy was getting organized. Somebody was giving sharp orders and apparently dividing the available men into three detachments. One group was already in pursuit of Starke and the girl. Now a second deployed into the woods in search of Diego. The remainder started to fight fire.

"Slow down," Starke called to Sue. "Don't risk getting hurt; we've got quite a distance to go."

"I can see," she panted. "That means they can see us. The light from the fire."

"We're almost out of it. By the time they get their men into the woods they'll be groping blind. They won't find us if they don't hear us."

He handed her the spare gun which he had been carrying, the one he had taken from the bewhiskered man. "Keep it handy. I'll reload this one."

"Second time you've given me a gun," she breathed. "It's getting to be a habit."

"This time you may have to use it. But be careful who you shoot at. Diego's around here somewhere. He lit the fire for us."

"Anybody else?"

"Just us. You'll have to take a share in the fighting if it comes to a shoot-out."

"I'm ready," she said grimly. "Do we keep on going in this same direction?"

"Straight on," he said. "Any direction is good so long as it's south."

CHAPTER
NINETEEN

It took some time to get away from the glare that was lighting the sky behind them. Starke guessed that the blaze had spread from the hay piles to the other supplies and was becoming a major conflagration. He said as much, trying to encourage Sue to keep moving. She made no complaint, just shoving on through the brush at his direction, finally emerging along the brook which led to their immediate goal.

"How much farther?" she gasped finally. "I'm getting winded."

"Three minutes — but slow down a bit if you want to. I don't think they're following us very closely. They'll hesitate about plunging into the woods in the dark. Probably start a real search when daylight comes."

"How long will that be?"

"Maybe an hour. No sign of gray in the east yet. Anyway we'll want to pick up Diego before we start to ride. With three of us we can put up a good fighting retreat."

They went on another fifty paces before she inquired, "Where in the world are we? I wasn't permitted to see where I was being taken."

He explained in some detail, describing the arrangements that had been made through McCall. "So maybe we won't have to fight our way all through to San Antonio. There's a good chance that help is on its way right now — even if they don't know just how much we need 'em."

She was silent for some time. Then she said, "I take it you tried your rescue attempt tonight in order to get me clear of what is likely to be a battleground. Is that it?"

"Something like that. Why? Did you think I was just swashbuckling again?"

Her nervous little giggle hinted at the strain she had been under, but her reply was steady. "That's exactly what I thought. I'm very contrite now. Really."

He slipped his arm about her, helping her along for the last fifty feet. "We have two horses," he explained. "My idea is that we'll have to lead them anyway until we get well clear of the hideout. I'll show the way until we strike the marked trail. Then you take the lead while Diego and I act as rear guard. Don't slow down if you hear shooting; just keep heading for open country. When you hit the first real road, turn left and ride hard for help."

"But what about you?"

"Don't worry about either of us. We'll stay right with you if it is possible. If the pressure gets too hot we'll cover your retreat. Diego and I have handled this sort of thing before; we'll take care of ourselves."

"I'd rather stay and help."

"Nobody gave you any choice. You obey orders, young lady."

"Yes, Lieutenant," she said meekly.

They had the horses ready to move when a rustle of leaves brought them to alert attention. There was a little gray seeping down out of the eastern sky now and Starke could make out the form of a man turning off from the brook trail. "Diego?" he called, gun held ready.

"Colonel Diego Menendez," the reply came in gleeful tones. "After tonight's performance I have just promoted myself. This has been more fun than I've had since the night I started the two companies of Imperials shooting at each other in the darkness. Did you get the lady clear away?"

"Without a hitch. We're just waiting for you to show up. Any sign of pursuit back there?"

"Not yet. They're still a little disorganized." A rattle of explosions from the direction of the blaze made Diego chuckle. "The hay makes a hot fire," he commented. "Now it seems to have spread to the ammunition. Maybe I should promote myself to General for such a fire."

"Very well, General. You and I bring up the rear. For the moment it's all yours because I need to show our advance guard how to find the trail out. Better get your guns ready; this next part won't be as easy as starting fires."

"You wound my pride," Diego complained. "But lead on. I am deflated and ready for work."

They were a good quarter of a mile along the guerrilla trail before the gray dawn could become real daylight. By that time Sue was leading both horses and the two men were together at the rear. Diego claimed that there had been no outlaw pickets posted along this trail; consequently, it seemed best to concentrate all fire power at the spot where the most likely attack might come.

Another quarter mile slipped behind without alarm; then they heard hoofbeats on the back trail. There was a chance that this might be simply a messenger going for help, a rider who might be avoided by ducking into the brush for a moment or two, but Starke didn't dare risk it. Better to keep moving toward the public road than to take a chance on being trapped.

"Same routine," he said briefly to Diego and both men took cover at either side of the trail. Sue followed orders and kept right on going.

They waited in complete silence, watching for any possible flankers, but the woods were silent. There was only the sound of hoofs on the trail itself. Then a line of men appeared, riding in single file. Starke counted six but could not be certain that there were not more behind them.

"Two apiece," he called softly to the Mexican. "Then run for it."

Again there was silence until the leader was not thirty feet from Starke's position. Carefully the ambusher's gun came up to draw fire on the stained gray shirt of the rider. Immediately the blast brought an echo from across the trail and Starke swung his weapon

226

to gun down the third man. Again he had his echo and he turned to run after Sue. It came as a mild annoyance to hear Diego blast a third shot.

This sort of ambush procedure had been practiced so often against marauding Imperials that the routine was thoroughly understood. Starke took the odd numbers, Diego the evens. It was always a case of fire and retreat together, counting on the sudden alarm to throw the enemy off stride.

"Sorry," Diego called as he ran up behind Starke. "One of them didn't get out of sight fast enough. I was tempted."

Starke didn't bother to discuss the matter. "Think there's any more coming up back there?"

"Not for a few minutes. I think these gentlemen were riding to order others into action in getting us surrounded. For the moment we have prevented that particular move."

"We can't hold it up long. They'll be smarter next time and we'll have to watch for some kind of circling tactics."

They ran on, neither wasting breath again until Diego panted, "Look! She's pointing at something."

Sue had halted in the trail, motioning ahead. Starke slowed his pace to listen and she called, "Someone coming toward us. We're caught between them."

There was definitely a sound of galloping horses coming in from the direction of the Fredericksburg road. Starke issued his orders quickly. "Into the brush. Get those ponies out of sight pronto! We'll stay with you this time, either for a fight or a fast run."

Unfortunately the woodland was thin at that point and before they could draw far enough back from the trail they could see a pair of horsemen coming around a bend. At the same moment the lead rider saw them and evidently realized that one was the escaping prisoner. He shouted something back along the line and instantly horses began to crash into the brush. One man kept right on going, as though to ride on toward the camp, but several of them were swinging in position to close in on the fugitives.

"Back to the trail," Starke ordered promptly. "We'll make a break for it. This time we'll ride. Can you hold on behind me, Sue?"

"Don't ask foolish questions!" she snapped back. "I can hold on with one hand and shoot with the other."

Starke was grabbing for a horse as he retorted, "Don't brag. You'll sound like Diego and we'll have to make you a colonel."

A slug crashed through the branches near him as he swung into the saddle. Diego fired in return and suddenly they were in the midst of a running battle. They made the trail without taking any injury and then it was once more a fighting retreat as the outmaneuvered enemy had to waste time getting back into the open. Starke was firing steadily now, trying to make sure that Diego would have time to reload. By changing off they could keep the pursuers pretty busy.

Suddenly they broke out into the relatively open space that he knew was the Fredericksburg road. As if on signal, the pursuit stopped. No longer were those riders trailing along to exchange fire; now they were riding directly away. Starke had no time to wonder about it. Even before he turned he heard Sue shouting.

She was pointing southward along the road to where a cavalry pennon fluttered above a mass of blue uniforms. Colonel Haney had made his move at just the proper time. That meant other squadrons coming in on the hideout from other directions. That last group of guerrillas must have been pickets coming in to give the alarm.

Two minutes later Starke was pulling up to speak with Captain Ritchie, a little bewildered at having the burly man salute him. "Is the fire at the outlaw hideout?" Ritchie asked, not even waiting to satisfy his evident curiosity about Sue.

"Diego fired the place as a diversion to let me get Miss Mallory out," Starke said. "I don't think you'll meet much resistance now. They're pretty badly rattled."

Ritchie saluted again and motioned for his troop to go on. He was a very businesslike officer and Starke wondered about him. This was not his regular command. Why was he here — and why was he getting so formal?

A rattle of gunfire from the brush hinted that Ritchie's column would not be the first to strike the guerrilla forces. Starke sat his bronc in silence for a moment before turning to his companions. "I think our share of the party is over, *compadres*. The army has taken over."

Sue was staring curiously after the disappearing troopers. "Duty certainly does make a machine of Ned Ritchie," she murmured. "He scarcely spoke to me."

"I don't imagine he quite knew how to take finding you here."

"No? Wasn't he looking for me?"

Starke grinned. "Sorry to deflate your ego, but the army was not out in search for a wandering officer's-brat. This attack on the outlaw roost was planned some days ago. It was only yesterday that Lily and his thugs decided to use you for bait."

"Bait? You certainly are complimentary — or else not! What do you mean?"

"Allow me," Diego cut in. "This part I claim leave to tell."

He told it with considerable enthusiasm and a certain amount of poetic liberty. Apparently he had sensed that the former relationship between Susan Mallory and Captain Ritchie had been definitely altered. At any rate, he told it that way, implying a different sort of romance.

Another body of troops appeared while he was talking and Starke motioned toward them. "Here comes Colonel Haney and some reserves. We should hear all of the answers pretty soon."

Actually, he had to give the answers for some time. Haney sent his men ahead while he stopped to trade information. Starke had to repeat practically all of what Diego had just covered for Sue, and if the girl noticed any differences in the two accounts she did not interrupt.

230

A trooper rode back to report, bringing word that most of the enemy had already been rounded up, practically without a fight. Some had evidently slipped off into the brush, but troops were now scouring the hills in search of them.

"I didn't ride back with the troops because I thought it would be this way," Starke told Haney. "Diego and his little box of matches put the whole gang out of business. Lily's dead, and with him out of the way I didn't think there would be much point in harrying the others too hard. The rank and file won't do much without leaders."

"Right enough. I hope we can pin something on Rose."

"I'll wager you don't have the opportunity," Sue said calmly. "I heard any number of remarks to the effect that he was the one who gave orders to have me seized. He'll disappear in a hurry when he learns how his bright scheme turned out. If he doesn't, I can testify against him."

"Two questions," Starke said. "What was Ritchie doing out here with one of the raiding squadrons? And why did he salute me so formally? Was he being sarcastic or something because he found Sue here with me?"

Haney's smile was quizzical. "That's three questions. I'll tackle only the first two. Captain Ritchie seemed to feel that he had made a mess of his other assignment. He learned of our plans and asked permission to lead one of the raiding parties. Second, he saluted you because he knew that you ranked him. Just before we left Fort Sam Houston we had word that you received two promotions during the war. You were made a captain after the consular service passed on a report of your first successful raids against Confederate supply lines. Promotion to your majority came less than a year ago. Evidently your career has not been overlooked at all. The records were simply not in the usual places and we didn't know what had happened until General Merritt's inquiries began to stir people up. My congratulations, Major Starke."

"Pooh!" Diego muttered. "Much too slow. I promoted myself twice already this morning." However, he reached out to shake the hand of his comrade-in-arms. "The only trouble with my promotions is that I won't have any extra pay to spend. You should have quite a lump coming."

Starke grinned, his glance darting toward Sue. "I think I know just how I can use it."

"Sorry we were so late with it," Haney said. "I didn't blame you for being rather bitter about the whole thing."

"It was well that it happened that way," Starke commented. "If I'd been a major instead of a lieutenant I might have blundered the other assignment just as Ritchie almost did."

"How do you mean?"

"Let me go back a bit. When I arrived in camp after my three years' absence from army routine, I was struck by one change of form that had taken place. Somewhere along the line it apparently had become the custom to call lieutenants mister. Other officers get their titles, but a lieutenant is just mister. So far as I can find out, that is true in the United States army only. The Confederates followed the European practice of giving rank titles all the way down.

"When this man who claimed to be Major Weldon pulled his bluff, he kept referring to me as Lieutenant. It made me wonder. When I started wondering, I got suspicious. He sounded like either a former Rebel or a Maximilian foreigner. In that case his game was obvious and I decided to gamble that he was the fake he seemed. He could have made the mistake with no other officer but a lieutenant."

"Apparently no one else noticed the error," Haney said dryly.

"No one else was so recently returned to army life that the habit would have been so noticeable."

"A modest swashbuckler," Miss Mallory proclaimed. "Now will someone do something about finding me a horse? I'm getting tired of hanging on back here with my arm so indecorously around the waist of a man who can't quite decide what his rank really is."

Starke wheeled his horse at once. "Field Marshal Diego Menendez!" he snapped. "You will proceed at once to guide Colonel Haney toward the site of the enemy headquarters. He'll want to interview prisoners and direct the mop-up details . . . and if you see anybody with a spare horse you might send him along so that I can be relieved of the extra load I'm carrying."

Haney and the Mexican grinned broadly as Starke turned in the saddle to lift Sue and swing her around in front of him. "Until that horse is forthcoming," he added, "I'll try to keep things as comfortable as possible."

Diego saluted briskly. "Within the week," he promised.

ISIS publish a wide range of books in large print, from fiction to biography. Any suggestions for books you would like to see in large print or audio are always welcome. Please send to the Editorial Department at:

ISIS Publishing Limited
7 Centremead
Osney Mead
Oxford OX2 0ES

A full list of titles is available free of charge from:

Ulverscroft Large Print Books Limited

(UK)
The Green
Bradgate Road, Anstey
Leicester LE7 7FU
Tel: (0116) 236 4325

(Australia)
P.O. Box 314
St Leonards
NSW 1590
Tel: (02) 9436 2622

(USA)
P.O. Box 1230
West Seneca
N.Y. 14224-1230
Tel: (716) 674 4270

(Canada)
P.O. Box 80038
Burlington
Ontario L7L 6B1
Tel: (905) 637 8734

(New Zealand)
P.O. Box 456
Feilding
Tel: (06) 323 6828

Details of ISIS complete and unabridged audio books are also available from these offices. Alternatively, contact your local library for details of their collection of ISIS large print and unabridged audio books.